Musings, Mutterings, and Aw Shucks

To Linda,
thanks for your interest
in my work

Elizabeth
4/26/12

Musings, Mutterings, and Aw Shucks

A Collection of Short Stories, Essays, and Features

BY

ELIZABETH CARROLL FOSTER

hteb963@suddenlink.net
www.elizabethcfoster.blogspot.com

iUniverse, Inc.
Bloomington

Musings, Mutterings, and Aw Shucks
A Collection of Short Stories, Essays, and Features

iUniverse books may be ordered through booksellers or by contacting:

iUniverse
1663 Liberty Drive
Bloomington, IN 47403
www.iuniverse.com
1-800-Authors (1-800-288-4677)

ISBN: 978-1-4620-5771-9 (sc)
ISBN: 978-1-4620-5773-3 (hc)
ISBN: 978-1-4620-5772-6 (ebk)

Printed in the United States of America

iUniverse rev. date: 12/15/2011

DEDICATION PAGE

These stories are dedicated to friends, acquaintances and those I did not know, all of whom spurred my imagination and unwittingly sparked the burning idea for a story. They are especially dedicated to all the writers who read, analyzed, and edited my work, and last but not least, to my husband John for his patience and support.

ACKNOWLEDGMENTS

To all those who listened, read, and analyzed the stories, "Thank you."

A special thanks to John Achor, Bill White, Danielle Burch, John Tailby, Pug Jones, Gene Heath, Judy Carroll, Linda Hamon, and Mary Ann Robertson. In addition, I must not leave out Madelyn Young, who proofread all of the stories. Thanks to all.

QUOTE PAGE

The rising with Aurora's light,
The Muse invoked, sit down to write.
Blot out, correct, insert, refine,
Enlarge, diminish, interline.

> Jonathan Swift (1667-1745)
> On Poetry (1733)
> 1.85

. . . and unto wizards that peep, and that mutter: . . .

> The Bible
> Isaiah 8:19

You will have written exceptionally well if, by skillful arrangement of your words, you have made an ordinary one seem original.

> Horace (65-8 B. C.)
> Ars Poetica
> 47

TABLE OF CONTENTS

PREFACE

ERATO, THE CREATIVE WRITER'S MUSE, perches on my shoulder at the oddest of times. Over the years, she invades my mind, planting seeds for new story ideas or works in progress.

Most of the tales in this collection are fictional short stories with a sprinkling of flash fiction. Other prose forms—essays and a feature—are set apart in the back of the book. Skipper, our family dog, Ozzie and Harriet, and our cats brought us much joy. Last, but not least, my teacher was my friend.

Some short stories are embellishments of my own experiences. Such as the outdoor religious service that happened when I was barely a teenager. My dad did buy a goose for Thanksgiving and cause my mother's problems in preparing it.

Versions of Daddy Joe's demise and *Seeking Christmas Joy* can be found in my novel, *Southern Winds A' Changing*. In addition, some Skipper capers are included in my memoir, *Follow Me: The Life and Adventures of a Military Family*.

Inspiration for some stories came during the Hemingway-Pfeiffer Creative Writers' Retreat held twice a year in Piggott, Arkansas. Recent ones are *Contemplating the Nippled Lemon, Sad is the Heart, Going to Piggott*, and the three flash fiction stories.

Ernest Hemingway once wrote, "All you have to do is write one true sentence. Write the truest sentence that you know." With that in mind, I wrote *Meed to a Pear Tree*.

Hemingway's second wife was Pauline Pfeiffer of Piggott, Arkansas. On visits to her family, the author wrote a few chapters of *A Farewell to Arms* in his barn studio provided by Pauline's father. Offered tours of the restored Pfeiffer-Janes home and the Barn Studio give interesting facts about the Hemingway family.

The Hemingway Creative Writers' Retreat happens bi-annually in the Education Center on the grounds of the Hemingway-Pfeiffer Museum. Dr. Rob Lamm, Arkansas State University, conducts the June retreat. Roland Mann—a former Marvell Comics editor, journalist, newspaper editor and now a talented author and creative writing instructor in Oxford, MS—conducts the November retreat. As our mentors, they and Diana Sanders the HP assistant director and retreat coordinator, with her assistant, Karen, and gift shop operator, Johnna, make the Hemingway Creative Writers' Retreat a place for scribes to bond, network and be creative. Long time and recently retired retreat coordinator Deanna Dismukes preceded Diana Sanders. Time at the retreat is well spent.

A few of the stories in this collection have won writing awards. I read some of them at our village Writers' L'Audible Art presentation. Our writer's club presents L'Audible Art once a year. Open to the public free of charge, wine and cheese is served in a setting reminiscent of the early Twentieth Century years when Scott Fitzgerald, Hemingway and other American writers were in Paris. Most of our scribes read one of their original works to an audience of 100-plus apparently appreciative listeners. Our audience returns each year, and it grows.

Our writers' club of between twenty-five to thirty supportive members, adds to the pleasure experienced in the writing process.

I enjoy delving into my imaginary worlds, and I hope my readers enjoy the experience of reading my work.

SHORT STORIES

Musings and Mutterings

DEVIL'S GONNA GET'CHA

A SOUTHWEST ARKANSAS EVENING HELD ONTO Hades-like heat as if it were a treasured condition. On this evening, a preacher came to the crossroad village to convince those gathered that they did not have to experience the real heat of Hades. More likely than not, his intention was to gather in the sheaves.

Under the heated sky, the preacher's outdoor gathering place faced the highway between two village stores. Some eight to ten women, at least a dozen of us young people and a handful of children trickled in to fill the temporary place to hear him speak. There was not a man among us to sit on the rows of rough planks spanning spaces between stacked cinder blocks. All the young men were off fighting World War II. Most of the older men worked in defense plants that took them away from home. Those still around probably resisted going to a religious service when it was not even a Sunday.

Whatever the men's reasons for not showing that evening, it was not hard to figure out why the mothers took center-row seats. They needed to keep an eye on their little tykes up front and an ear to us misbehaving teenagers on the back row.

Even before the preaching began, we young people jabbed each other in the ribs and joked about the ordained man wiping sweat from his brow and pacing back and forth in front of his audience as though wearing his thinking cap. We committed sacrilege. At least we knew our Sunday school indoctrination and mothers' training deemed it sacrilege.

3

Soon our attention focused on Miss Elsie Waylock. She stretched up on her tippy-toes and plopped down in the middle of a center-row bench. The distance between the end blocks did not allow for a lot of plank sag caused by Miss Elsie's weight. Heedless of the sag, she crossed her fat little feet and dangled them above the ground.

Mr. Thompson did not give Miss Elsie one word of warning about the danger of the plank cracking at any minute. He just handed her one of his cardboard fans attached to popsicle-like sticks. The fans, meant to cool us, were a fine advertisement for his store.

Reaching our back row, he did not seem to notice the ripple of uncontrollable sniggers snuffled behind our hands. Jimmy Hickok just could not stop his outburst over Miss Elsie's peril.

His mama stood up, marched back to where he sat and whopped him up beside the head with her purse. Mrs. Hickok wore her hair rolled from earlobe to earlobe over a net tube and held in place with hairpins. I remembered her face in no other shape than a scowl.

Whopping Jimmy was not the thing to do. "Ha, ha, ha" erupted from the rest of us.

"Come with me, Jimmy." Mrs. Hickok pulled her son up by the ear and stomped off behind the store building.

"Ouch, Mama. Okay, okay, I will," came from that direction.

Leading him back by the ear, they sat side-by-side for the service. Jimmy looked back at us, showing his dispiritedness. Then, one glance at Miss Elsie contorted his face into stifled giggles again, and his mama glared at him.

Miss Elsie seemed content with herself. She swished her fan back and forth to bring a faint breeze to her face. Did she pretend not to hear our commotion going on behind her?

Mrs. Larson turned and gave her son a look scathing enough to wilt daisies. To Miss Elsie directly behind her, she said, "Elsie, maybe you ought . . . uh, you ought to sit near the end of the bench."

Before Miss Elsie could move, the pew cracked.

"Oh great gravy! Miss Elsie's fallen from grace," Jimmy yelled.

The back row broke into loud guffaws as though we gave not one thought to Miss Elsie's misery, as she lay sprawled in the dirt between two pieces of broken plank.

Mrs. Hickok whopped Jimmy up beside the head again then joined others gathered around the dear woman. Struggling to roll over, Miss Elsie found it impossible, and Mrs. Hickok made a frantic grab at her print dress. She jerked it down over her distraught friend's exposed thighs. The other women clucked like hens over their neighbor. Then, helping the preacher pull her upright, they almost dumped Miss Elsie again before getting her settled.

"Oh good gravy!" Jimmy could not help himself. He looked back at us and whispered, "This time the *preacher* almost dropped her from grace."

We nudged each other, laughing aloud, until Mrs. Hickok came to the back, and stood in front of us with a glare of authority.

Despite her threat, it took some time to quiet our escaping giggles. Images still played in my mind's eye. Once the shuffling around the poor flustered soul stopped, the women's expressions of sympathy and our giggles quieted. Miss Elsie sat on a safer seat, and the preacher stood before his flock. He rolled up the sleeves of a sweaty white shirt clinging to his expansive paunch, unbuttoned it at the neck and pulled his necktie askew. Tucking the Bible underarm and thumbs under dark suspenders, Brother Crowley strutted back and forth before us. He took us down into the fiery pits of Hell and lifted us heavenward again.

Nevertheless, it was hard to hold us in either place for reality kept interfering.

Purrs of approaching automobiles and accompanying "cracks" and "pops" of gravel against metal caused Brother Crowley to turn toward the sounds and spit a string of Day's Work Tobacco juice. As the road dust swirled on the heavy air, he made a complete circle, watching each car fade from sight. "Amen," he shouted, never missing a beat in the sermon, except for the time to expectorate.

Few cars came along the road—the war and all—but enough, considering the dust. Caught there in the swirl, between Heaven and Hell, Mrs. Hickok's glare at Jimmy clearly indicated what awaited him for being disrespectful to Miss Elsie and the preacher. When the preaching ended, some of the mommas shook their heads and agreed with one's remark, "The devil's going to get them sooner than later."

In all likelihood, deep down in our young souls, we feared a fiery hell. If not, we could be almost certain when our mothers got us home, they would plant several kinds of fear in us.

DODD TELLS
ABOUT DADDY JOE'S DEATH

LFREEDA LEFT BROTHER JAMES TO linger with his flock and came over where I waited. We took Nate's hands and walked away from the Sunday churchgoers.

Yesterday, she and the preacher visited us on the DeWitt farm. They brought Nate and me to spend the rest of the weekend with them. Last night, I helped Elfreeda make most of our Sunday dinner. Now, crossing the street to the James' house, she picked up my son and over her shoulder said, "Hurry on, Maizee, dinner should be on the table when the preacher gets here."

Shortly, he joined us and following his "amen" after grace, I heard a rap at the door.

Elfreeda looked in my direction. "It's Dodd Turner. He comes about ever Sunday for my fried chicken." She yelled, "Come on in, Dodd."

Chairs scraped around the table, tightening the circle to make room for him. Sliced tomatoes, green peas, gravy, and biscuits rising two inches high passed from hand to hand. My Nate reached for the fried chicken. I told him to wait, and put a wing on his plate. All the dishes made a round of the table, and soon talk turned to guessing about the death of the white man to be buried that afternoon. Dodd chewed and grunted his liking of the food. No one acted as if anything else was expected from him, when all of a sudden he up and said, "I'll tell you exactly what happen to Mista Joe."

Elfreeda jumped as if struck by a lightning bolt. Brother James stopped in mid-chew, and I didn't understand the interest in the old dead man at all. Dodd held a chicken thigh before gapped teeth, ready to bite into it, and Nate gnawed on a wing and imitated the old man's satisfied grunts.

After a few more grunts, Dodd saw plainly that he had everybody's attention. "He's called Daddy Joe by his kids, you know. Well, I be sitting in front of my store when Mista Joe DeWitt passed in his car on Friday evening." Dodd took a bite and chewed, then, "He do it all the time, you know, going over to Vickery's. Like always, he gets outta the car with a bottle of Jim Beam whiskey in a brown paper sack. Like he's hiding it." Dodd giggled.

"How long this been going on?" He looked at Elfreeda and laughed way down in his throat. "Twelve or more years? Since Miss Berniece died. Ever Friday, jest like clockwork."

Everybody but Nate chewed slow-like as we watched Dodd pluck another piece of chicken off the platter before he went on.

"Anyways, Vickery done been over to the store to get liver. She makes U'Orleans style liver with rice for him when I can get liver." Dodd chuckled, low and garbled through a mouthful of food. "Makes you wonder what that old white man saw in that shriveled up old colored woman."

Elfreeda giggled, and Brother James flipped his red polka-dotted necktie over his shoulder. He struggled to look real stern, but it was plain he tried hard not to laugh.

Me, I'm watching his problem get bigger and make a little giggle of my own. I clamped a hand over my mouth, cause I thought about the day I would have to tell my Nate that the dead man was his old white granddaddy. I wiped Nate's cheek on my napkin and wondered if anyone at the table knew that Quentin DeWitt raped me in the cotton shed on the Dewitt Farm.

"Maizee, do you know Vickery?" Elfreeda jolted me back to what Dodd had said. "Vickery lives next door to Dodd. He lives in the back of his store." She turned to Dodd, fanning with her napkin. "We don't care about her cooking, Dodd. Get on with it."

The breeze coming through the kitchen window did not move the heat left in the cook stove. We were all hot and fanning with our napkins.

"Well," Dodd started up again, "I been over there many a time after supper. Them two be listening to the radio. You know, Amos and Andy . . . and having shots of Jim Beam."

Brother James' eyes flashed heavenward. "Lawd! Lawd!"

Dodd didn't pay any mind to the reverend's calling on The Above. "Well, apparently they got to romping in bed later on, cause about three-thirty in the morning, Vickery come a pounding on my door. 'It's Vickery, Dodd! Come quick!' She says it over and over in a squeaky voice, afraid she gonna wake up ever'body."

Uneasy about what he might say next, I am shifting on my chair and pulling at the puffed sleeves of my Sunday dress.

"Well," Dodd said, "I get up and open the door. I be in my drawers and she's standing there in a white nightgown. If I hadn't knowed her, I would a thought she was a ghost." Words slid over his tongue like molasses dripping from the half-eaten biscuit he held ready for another bite. He peered around the table at us from under his crumpled old hat and chomped into the biscuit. Then he took a chicken wing off the platter.

Elfreeda had hardly touched her food. Sitting on the edge of her chair, she said, "Man, you gonna get to what happened or ain'cha?"

"I'm getting there, Freeda. Well, we run in to Vickery's house, and there was Mista Joe face down on her bed, naked as a baby bird and dead as a doornail."

"Lawd, Lawd." The preacher shook his head.

Again, his calling made not a dent on Dodd. "Vickery say, 'Help me get him outta here.' Her itty-bitty eyes be full a fright. She be white already, being a mulatto and all, now she done gone gray. I be scared, too." Dodd eyes flared wide open, leaving a lot of white in his black face.

Taking a bite of chicken, he chewed and swallowed before going on. "We like to never got Mista Joe's underwear and pants on. Vickery slip one arm in his shirtsleeve and me the other. We latched his suspenders in back and rolled him over to latch em in front. Then we pull that heavy body by the feet so it hangs mostly off the bed. Man! You know what happen then?"

Potatoes dropped from Nate's spoon, and he held a drumstick as we all leaned over the table.

"That dead man slid off the bed." Dodd dropped a chicken bone on his plate.

Nate went bug-eyed, and Elfreeda drew tight as strung wire, straining a button on her red frock. She looked molded in place with a partially eaten piece of chicken dangling from her hand.

Brother James and me patted Nate's arm and waited on Dodd to get on with his tale.

It was plain we all had an appetite for more, so he told us how they finished dressing the man's dead body. "Vickery stands back and inspects. See if anything left undone. Then she jerks up a patchwork, flaps it and lets it fall to the floor beside the body. We roll him on the quilt and pull him through the front room on to the porch."

Dodd grimaced. "We standing there, breathing so heavy it hurt to gulp air. We look like goblins under that moon shining bright as day."

His eyes were big and shiny in the kitchen shadow when he took up his story again. "We listening to see if anybody spying on us. Some alley cats be meowing a few doors up. Vickery whispers, 'Anybody hear us, maybe they think I be going to the privy.'" Dodd giggled. "Anyways, we pull that body off the porch on to the ground, and I say, 'What we gonna do now?' Vickery say, 'Put him in the car, and you gonna drive down on the highway and head it in the ditch. He gonna look like he died behind the steering wheel.'"

Dodd said he told Vickery he would be in a heap of trouble if white folks found out Mista Joe died in her house instead of the car. "She say, 'Shut yo mouth, man! You be in trouble anyways if they know you helped to move him.'" Dodd shook his head. "There didn't seem to be any other way. I was already in too deep. We do exactly like Vickery say."

Dodd's predicament had Elfreeda and me laughing tears, and Nate snickering behind his hands. Then I remembered the dead man was Nate's old white granddaddy. Could I tell Elfreeda about Nate before we went home? Maybe when it came time, she could help me talk to Nate.

"Ahem." Brother James cleared his throat, and I knew we had been disrespecting a dead man. Our laughing came unwound around the table like a rolling ball of yarn.

A DOG AND HIS MAN

$\mathscr{B}$RANDON RAN AHEAD, HIS NOSE to the ground and tail wagging with growing excitement. The golden retriever stopped and looked back, waiting for Paul who sat astride his horse Spade. Brandon panted a dog smile up at his master. Nothing could top an outing with his friend.

Dog, man, and horse moved along the path beside the Maryland stream. It was of no concern to Brandon that the run had no special name. To him it meant a place for him, Paul and Spade to explore.

Before his master went away, he and Paul explored the run often. Understanding Paul's many months of absence fell beyond him, and he spent much of that time lying on the front porch, waiting and longing for his friend. He longed for the days when his strong young man reined-in Spade beneath a shade tree, swung a leg up on the saddle and drew in the scents of autumn olive and holly blooms. In those pre-war days, though eager to explore with his nose, Brandon showed patience when Paul lingered. Now, his patience was more important than ever.

When his companion returned, right away Brandon sensed something different about him. Welcoming him home with licks, tail wags and sniffing, Brandon picked up no scent or warmth when touching his cold nose to one of Paul's legs. He didn't want to rub against it, or place his head on it when Paul lay back on the grassy stream bank. His master did not wrestle on the carpet in a toy-take-away game or romp outside anymore.

From day one of his return, Brandon stayed near his pal, making sure abandonment did not happen again. If his friend stopped to bird watch, lean over the bridge rail with a fishing pole, or heft his game leg around to pick blackberries, he would be there beside him.

Today, he sat on the path, panting and waiting for Paul and Spade to catch up. When Paul reined in his horse and looked out on patches of yellow black-eyed Susans and cornflower blue chicory, Brandon waited, sensing his friend had missed this place.

Gazing up at Paul, he cocked an ear, and it was all right with him that those colors didn't catch his eye. His nose told him what was on the trail, and all that mattered was being with Paul. Both stared at the clear blue sky, watching a hawk soar and screech for some reason unknown to Brandon. Sniffing the air, he glanced at Paul and waited for him to relay a rush of urgency. Sensing none, he turned an ear to bird sounds emanating from the woods, put his nose to the ground and trotted forward. This nowhere-place teemed with life and delighted his quivering nose.

His nose told him much flushing-out waited in the grass, at the tree roots and in the creek. Small animals rustled through dry leaves and grasses to scurry beneath undergrowth, prompting him to run after them. Large and small insects crawled across his path on the way to somewhere, stopping him in his tracks.

Coming up to him, Paul called, "What did you find, boy?"

Brandon looked up at his master with a wag of his tail that meant the find was not significant, then, he trotted on alongside Spade.

Soon, Paul dismounted. Brandon waited as he hitched up his blue jeans and tightened his belt. Unaware Paul had been in Iraq, he sensed changes in his man's body and leg, but he didn't care. His master was back with him.

Paul walked with him to the edge of the creek. A snake slithered into the water. Brandon did not want to tangle with it. There was no indication from Paul that he should, and they watched it swim downstream. Water gurgled over large stones in the creek bed and seemed to hold his master's attention. That was okay with Brandon. He waited at Paul's side, sensing his friend's need to be at peace with nature and himself—a need they shared.

"It's a nice fall day, boy."

Brandon watched him remove his cap and replace it without awareness that his friend's hair shed like falling leaves. He followed Paul back up on the path.

Trotting ahead, panting his happy smile, he stopped to wait. Turning, he saw Paul lie down in the shade of a willow tree and bounded back to sit beside him. Minutes passed as he relished Paul's strokes on his furry back. A heavy stillness fell around them. Paul's hand rested on his back, and Brandon heard noises coming from him. He tried to stay awake, but his eyes grew heavy too.

Suddenly, Brandon woke to Paul's movement. He buried his face in Brandon's furry coat and mumbled words that meant nothing to Brandon. His master lifted on his elbow, wiped his eyes and uttered "Nightmares, boy"—words the retriever didn't understand. Then, he lay back on the bed of grass.

Brandon nudged against him and placed his head on Paul's chest, wanting to comfort him. After some passing of time, he sat up, waiting for a signal.

Paul roused, rolled on his side and pushed up on his warm leg. "It could be a bit cooler, boy." He removed his cap, wiped the inside rim and replaced it on his head. Back on the path, Brandon welcomed Paul's laugh and roughing up of his fur. "You know who comes a courting here, Brandon? Young boys come with their sweethearts. They are ready and able to impress their girls. I ain't likely to find a girl that will look twice at a guy with an artificial leg."

Sensing his sadness, Brandon looked up at him. What did Paul want him to do?

"Let's go, boy." Paul hitched the prosthesis forward.

They moved along the path, then Paul stopped. Someone had dumped a washing machine in the run. "This may be a nowhere place, but it's our place, Brandon."

The dog liked the sound of his name coming from his master. Catching a scent, Brandon stopped panting and raised his nose, sniffing the air. His man clasped a hand over his nose, mumbling something. Brandon ran over to a small tree. He knew the scent of a dead deer.

"I swear, boy. Sometimes, man acts like the lowliest of all creatures."

Brandon nudged his master's hand.

Suddenly, he caught sight of a duck gliding toward the water. Taking a hunter's stance, one paw braced in the air, he watched other ducks quack overhead and come in for a landing. Bounding off in an upstream direction, he disappeared down the creek embankment. In a few seconds, a quacking din sounded as he flushed the fowl back into the air.

Paul approached as Brandon rushed up onto the path with a mouthful of feathers. Watching the ducks rise above the low tree line, he shook his head. "No duck today, boy. Come on, this ain't a hunting day. It's just a day for me and you to be together."

Seeing Paul head for his horse, the retriever sensed the end of their exploring time. He sat down beside Spade and watched Paul place his foot in the stirrup and swing hard to heave the leg-with-no-smell over the saddle. "Come on, Brandon," he said, giving Spade a light spur.

Ever alert to any moving thing, Brandon trotted along beside Paul and Spade, walking his best friends back the way they had come. As long as his master did not care that the duck eluded him, Brandon was not disappointed.

A DAY IN THE LIVES OF THE MACLEOD'S

BESSIE LEANED ON THE KITCHEN counter holding the remote phone to her ear. She giggled into it, unmindful of rising smoke and grease popping from the skillet. When Bo walks in, she thought, I will say something to make him suspicious.

Brian Macleod answered to Bo, and Bessie thought it fitted her husband's image to a tee.

A muffled shout came from the bedroom. Bo often called her name for no obvious reason at all, but just in case he had some kind of difficulty, she tiptoed to the bedroom door and peeped around. Bo staggered about, pulling a sleeveless tee shirt over his head. Grabbing his dingy, billed cap from the bedpost, he started for the hallway, and Bessie high-stepped back to the kitchen.

Shoving the skillet from the heat, she flipped the stove burner off, fanned smoke, and coughing, flung open the door. She turned back, but Bo wasn't seated at the table. Bessie peered into the hallway.

He stood before the hall mirror with a diagonal crack running across it. With the cap at a slight angle over his baldness, black letters spelling Blatz Beer above the bill were barely discernable. The Milwaukee brewers closed their business in 1959, but Bo still wore the topper as a token of remembrance. He grinned at his reflection. Turning sideways before the mirror, he adjusted the angle of his cap and pulled at his sleeveless tee shirt. "Damn, you're good-looking." Turning from side to side, he surveyed the

14

tattoos on his upper arms. A red heart broke into jagged halves made by an arrow. The other, heart-shaped too and blue in color, read, "I love Mama."

Seemingly satisfied with his appearance, he bellowed "Bessie!" again and started toward the kitchen.

Bessie pulled away from the hall door and mumbled into the phone, "My old man doesn't suspect a thing. Bye." Satisfied their day had begun routinely, she placed the phone down on the table and turned to Bo.

"Where's breakfast?" he demanded, plopping down on a chair. "What's all the smoke and smell in here? You burned up the bacon like always."

"Breakfast is in the oven, honey. The bacon got a little crisp." Reaching into the oven, she complained, "Ouch! Plate's hot."

"Yeah, I'll bet it's hot enough to put a skirt on my eggs." Bo turned to her backside as she bent to close the oven door and gave her a full-hand pinch.

"Oh, you are a rascal. Had you rather have your eggs cold and on the floor?" Smiling above his head, Bessie slid the plate before him.

"Aren't we clever this morning? How long you been on that phone? What is it that I'm not supposed to suspect?" Bo slivered his knife through brown, curled edges of the egg whites, making screechy sounds.

The chalkboard noise set Bessie on end, and she let loose a word unfit to repeat, then, "Here's your coffee." Passing the cup across his plate, it rattled on the saucer and hot liquid sloshed over the rim.

"Watch out!" Bo dropped his knife in a brownish puddle and stared down at it. "Look at that! You spilled coffee all over my eggs!"

"I'll make more eggs," Bessie said, picking up his plate.

"Who was on the phone, Bess? You don't get calls this early."

"You wouldn't be interested."

Bo sighed. "Beats me. Gosh darn, can't you women find better to do than gossip?"

Bessie smiled over the frying pan. "Like what? Coddling your eggs to keep them warm?"

That zinger pleased her. She did not often voice something that clever. Placing the cooked to perfection eggs on his plate, she knew she had Bo on a tear today and thought to give it another stab. "What if I wasn't talking to a woman?"

Cutting into the sunny sides-up, Bo smiled without appearing to hear her remark. He chewed the last bite of egg, tore off a piece of toast, swiped

15

it around his plate and stuck it in his mouth. Swallowing, he reached for a toothpick and stood.

Bessie watched him head for the living room. She heard air swoo-osh out of the vinyl cushion as he flopped down on his recliner. The television came alive, and she visualized his hand welded to the remote control.

As she went about cleaning the kitchen, putting in a load of laundry and swishing a feather duster about, it pleased her that she had even mildly provoked Bo. Soon, she noticed the clock showed eleven thirty. Setting lunch on the table, she went to the living room to summon Bo.

He punched the off button on the remote and followed her back to the kitchen. "Hey, Bess, maybe you better tell me who the man is?"

"I didn't think you cared."

They stared across the table at each other.

"I care that some guy talks to *my* wife at seven o'clock in the morning. You don't want me to know, do you?"

"Oh, for heaven's sake, it was Tom. You wouldn't know him, Bo."

He bellowed, "Tom who?" and Bess told him Tom was just an old friend. "I went out with him a few times when—"

"What business does he have calling here?"

Thinking she finally had her couch potato in a stew, she said, "He's still my friend. What's wrong with a call from an old frien—"

"How long have these *friendly* calls gone on? Never mind! Your face is flushed red. You've been seeing this fathead!" Bo stood and paced, his lunch seemingly forgotten. He kicked the smelly old basset hound that followed him everywhere.

"Suppose I have. What's it to you, Brian MacLeod? The one who says, 'Bring me another beer, Bess,' from his sprawled position in front of the TV. Football, baseball, wrestling! You don't need a wife. All you need is a TV and a bartender."

He said she sounded like a fishwife, and Bess reminded him, "This fishwife made lunch for you. Are you going to eat?" She stared up at him and imagined steam oozing from his ears. She wondered what more she could say to keep the game going. Then it came to her. "Listen, Bo, what claim do you have? This place looks like a pig sty."

He sat at the table again and pounded it with his fist.

"Sure, pound the table to splinters. Please put the splinters in your beer cans." Those remarks brought a pause, then, "Why can't we ever go out?"

"Go out! Ah, Bess, you drag around here in that old robe and slippers, your hair not combed all day. Go out!" He bit into his sandwich.

Oh, we are going at it now, she thought, then, "What's the good of me getting all dolled up? Do you ever notice? All you care about is when your meal is ready and if a can of beer is opened." She chewed and swallowed. "Tom—"

"Tom what? If he could see you now! Ha! He wouldn't likely—"

"You old fool!" Bessie pointed her finger at Bo. "You're a danged old fool!"

"Fool! You made me sound like a fool on the phone. You little two-timing . . . You've been seeing him!"

She stood and took their plates to the sink. "Don't shout, Bo. I'm not deaf."

He rose slowly. "Okay, I'm leaving. Don't wait up for me."

"Oh, I won't, sweetie. You can't be rid of me that easily." As he banged the kitchen door behind him, Bessie knew exactly what to expect. She sat, eyes on the door as it eased open.

Bo stuck his head around it, grinning like a Cheshire cat. "That was a good one, Bess. Do you think we did it for today?"

"If that game didn't stir up our blood, we'll have another go-round later," she said. "There is nothing like a good round to get our old tickers pumping."

Laughing, they walked into the front room. Bessie picked up her half-read romance novel, plopped her hefty rear end on the couch and swung her feet onto the piled up coffee table.

Bo flopped back in his chair and took a slug of beer. "This one's warm, Bess. I need a cold one."

She sighed, happy that it was just another day in the Macleod's household.

CONTEMPLATING THE NIPPLED LEMON

AITING FOR ANDREW, HER SERVER, to bring iced tea, Sarah gazed at the green bowl in the middle of her table. It held fruit stacked into a peak. The yellow lemon on top projected a large, hard nipple on one end. It reminded her of a mother's breast.

Her waiter brought the glass of tea to her sidewalk table and set a small bowl of sliced lemon beside it. "A refreshing tea should lift that sadness I see on your face, Mrs. Kinley. It's been there a while, but I hope you enjoy this beautiful spring day." Turning to take another order, Andrew said over his shoulder, "Signal if you need a refill."

A frequent occupant of the same table, Sarah and Andrew shared a friendly repartee.

Though he distracted her for a moment, she found it difficult to erase an image the nippled lemon evoked and the sad memory it aroused. The beauty of her baby's chubby cheeks as she nourished at the breast filled Sarah's mind. Tiny trusting fingers curled around hers.

Placing the white napkin over her denim-covered lap, she pushed back an unruly strand from her forehead. How have I presented myself during the last ten months and twenty-one days? Devin never makes note of my slovenly disregard for dress and frowzy hair. Trying to draw me out of the foggy scene my life has become, he says we are still young. Begs me to remember the joy little Libby brought to our lives. He tells me how blessed we will be to have more babies.

All these months, Sarah thought, his words have fallen on my unheeding ears.

Gazing at the fresh fruit, she recalled her thoughts earlier that morning. Just for a moment, she felt grief had grabbed too much of her life. Felt it was time to live again.

Now, sitting at her table and turning the chilled glass between her hands, Devin's words grabbed her right down in her depths. Whom have I mourned all these months? Whom do I mourn now? Libby . . . or myself?

Sarah took a lemon slice from the small white bowl, squeezed it and licked her fingers. Tartness left her lips puckery. The sensation surprised her, and she licked her lips again for the lemon zest. She pondered the acerbic quality and wondered if a lemon could feel. If it feels, then what should I do? It had life before plucked from the tree. Had it felt the steel blade slice through its flesh? Had it felt a violation of its exotic being only for its many uses? How can it look viable?

Her questions provoked more thoughts.

Sarah picked up another slice, squeezed it and listened to the juice trickle onto the ice cubes. The tinkling sound presented an image of life's blood flowing from the lemon's cells, robbing it of nourishment. Holding a slice up to the sun allowed light to infuse its spoke-like segments and project a kaleidoscope of pale yellow, darker yellow, and tans. Like a Tiffany lamp, she thought.

The clean citrus scent drifted upward to fill her nostrils. What would it feel like to peel back the thick rind and squirt the pure liquid over my face? People will think I am loony. Maybe I am.

Then, choosing one perfectly formed lemon from the bowl, she rolled it around in her hand. It felt hard and thick-skinned, and she pictured her mother rolling lemons to make them supple for juicing. Sarah remembered her mother's lemon pies were delectable enough to make waiting for dessert almost unbearable.

Pulling out of the reverie, she reminded herself to concentrate on the sunny nature of the lemon. After all, its dimpled skin is the color of sunshine on this spring day. It is longwearing . . . like the lambskin handbag I carried for years.

What happened to that handbag? Unable to remember, she went on pondering the lemon.

Like this fruit, what is my purpose for being in this place at this time? Perhaps the lemon knows its function in the scheme of things. Knows it is meant to nourish people and be of use in many ways.

Suddenly, the lesson broke through, and Sarah knew she must accept conflicts and sad events as part of serving time given to her. Like the lowly lemon, she could nourish others . . . and for certain Devin, her beloved husband. Yes, they would have more babies.

Standing, Sarah thanked Andrew and walked down the street tossing the nippled lemon from hand to hand and smiling into a different day.

GETTING THE STORY

MY PATIENCE WANED AFTER AN hour of waiting near the food court when a young woman hurried past my bench seat in the mall corridor. She fit Megan's description of Lisa.

If it were Lisa, her six-year-old son Patrick trailed a good ways behind her, his eyes set on a colorful balloon tied to a baby stroller pushed alongside him. The distance between the young mother and her son in the crowded place concerned me. Many times I had observed mere tots lagging far behind a parent. It can lead to children snatched in broad daylight, I thought.

Mingling food odors and noisy Christmas shoppers made me question why I put myself through this to get a story.

Keeping an eye on Lisa, the person I hoped to interview, I recalled my conversation with Megan the day before. She had walked into the newsroom as I gathered up papers before going to a computer station to research the Internet for my feature. Flopping down behind her desk next to mine, Megan drew an exasperated breath, probably meant to get my attention. She had come from the park, a place she visited to feed the waterfowl and unwind from the day's tension.

Megan scooted her chair toward me, pulled long red curly hair over the shoulder, and wiped her face with a tissue. I noticed the summer sun had melted her freckles into each other.

Settling down, she said, "Those three kids showed up again today and threw stones at the ducks." On other occasions, she had told of seeing the same boys, two about eight and the other one maybe a year younger, casting rocks at the waterfowl. She had seen them bully smaller children on the park playground as well.

I knew her dander was up and she wanted to talk about it.

"If they were mine, I would whip their butts. Let them know what it feels like to have a stone bruise." The boys stood in the water's edge when a young woman sat down on the bench beside Megan. "Suddenly, she startled me when she yelled, 'Patrick, get out of the water. Now!'"

The youngest of the three, a towhead, stepped onto the grassy bank showing the wet legs of rolled-up jeans. Megan had broken into her story to tell of park rules against going into the water.

Guessing the girl beside her was the kid's mother, Megan asked if Patrick was her son. My nosy friend said she hoped to sound casual. "Does he want to feed the ducks?" she had asked, thinking she might make a connection between mother, child, and nature.

"He hates them. Doesn't like any kind of animal," the young woman said.

Megan got the idea the girl—not much older than her own daughter—did not wish to make a connection with her. "One of those generational things, you know." She laughed, drew on her cigarette and blew a stream of smoke toward the ceiling. She gave me a quizzical glance, and added, "They look at you as if thinking they don't ever want to look like you. Thinking they won't ever." She had wished the girl would say something like that so she could respond with a Roseanne Barr quip. "You know something like, 'Well, Darlene, I see your screw-ups etched in that tight little face already, and there's nothing like screw-ups to speed up your turning into a clone of your mother.' I don't know what Roseanne would say, but something like that."

Megan had laughed and held the cigarette away from me as though protecting my hair and clothing from the odor already permeating the smoke-filled newsroom. She had tried to give up the habit, but said, "It's as hard as ducks hanging bottoms-up and feeding underwater."

Gutsy like Roseanne, her weird sense of humor and understated wisdom made Megan a rough-cut gem in my eyes.

Continuing her encounter with the girl at the lake, Megan introduced herself but gained only a first name. "Lisa, that's her name." She took another puff on the cigarette. "I complained about the boys stoning the ducks. Well, when I did, Lisa yelled at the kid, 'Come here. Now, Patrick!' When the skinny little dude stood in front of his mother, she leaned forward, smacked him across the cheek and screamed, 'Don't throw rocks at the damned ducks.'"

Megan said she heard her own mother shouting and felt the swat of her hand. "Don't, Megan! Stop that, Megan!" For a moment, my friend had appeared lost in time, then, "A lot has changed since I was a kid, but does Lisa ever hear the echo of her mother? That kind of interaction between parents and children seems to be passed from generation to generation."

She said Patrick just stood there looking at his mother in a way that gave Megan the willies. "Not a look of physical pain. More baneful than that, it was as if he wanted to slap her back." She said he did not shed a tear but stood with that look pinned on his mother's face. "I had caused the kid pain, and I felt like crying. I do not know why, because I don't like the sneaky, brazen little brat. Can't help wondering how he'll turn out."

Again, Megan fell into that backward look.

Recovering from the past, she had suggested Lisa as a possible source for my feature story on single working mothers. She refused to set an interview for me, but she filled in details learned from her conversation in the park.

Lisa hung out with friends in the mall's food court, where she ate with Patrick on weekend nights. She worked as a server during the day. Megan mused over the girl's declaration that she would not eat from the food stall where she worked. "She's not married, and I suspect she never was, but she's looking for a guy. You can tell."

She learned that Lisa's father was in the military. "There's something quirky about that," Megan said. "From what I've read—well, there's Pat Conroy's book, *The Great Santini*—military fathers keep a tight rein on their kids. Lisa impresses me as a loose cannon."

There in the newsroom, Megan had done most of the talking and I had listened, agreeing Lisa sounded like a good source for my story. "It must be tiring for a single parent to wait tables all day and come home to mothering," I said. "I think my patience would fade quickly."

At that point, Frank, our editor, walked out of his glassed-in, open-door office into the newsroom. Some of the reporters said he always carried a look of knowing a lot about everything. When he thought he had gained advantage over one of us, a little grin played around his mouth, inviting a punch to his face. One news hound had said his ego was as big as his girth.

Megan's voice had a loud, hoarse quality that had allowed him to overhear our conversation. I knew he was about to interject himself. He often did.

Just as I thought, he leaned against the doorframe at the end of my desk and said, "Women have no business working. Their place is in the home, taking care of babies and husbands. You hear stuff about needing two salaries. That's a bunch of crap." The half-grin had worked around his sixty-year-old mouth. That grin always left me guessing whether he dared contradiction from us or thought he expressed an element of profundity. He jumped on the case of any missed story, no excuses allowed. Most of us stepped around Frank, having as little as possible to do with him.

From the look on her face, I recognized Megan's desire to knock Frank flat. "I'm out of here," she had announced. Policing up reporter's pad from her desk and tossing it into a big shoulder bag, she walked out, abandoning me to deal with Frank.

"Look around," he went on, "women don't have to work in the 1990's. You see all those cars, boats and travel vehicles parked in driveways. Do you see anyone poorly dressed today, or wearing the same clothing day after day? I had one suit when I started out and I wore it every day. You don't see people in scrubby shoes. Kids want a new pair of sixty-dollar sneakers every month. They get every new toy that comes to Toys R Us®. They're spoiled."

"That's a debatable subject, Frank." I turned back to my work in progress, hoping he would go away so I could finish and stop for the day.

However, he did not leave without delivering his punch lines. He said young people today want everything right now. They want sex without marriage then run around with kids that have no fathers. "They want everything without the responsibility that goes with having it. Why do you think there's so much crime in these times?"

I told him I could not think about all those things right now, and he walked off chortling.

He played out scenes like this numerous times, and I always wondered why he insisted on presenting an image that made us perceive him as overbearing. Was there another side to him? I recalled other times when he took seemingly unreasonable and adamant stands. Was he playing devil's advocate with me?

Frank's words passed through my mind as I watched Lisa's black mini-skirted figure plow through the rush of mall shoppers. From Megan's description, she had to be the target of my scheme. With reporter's pad in hand, I rose from the bench and followed in her direction.

Edging toward the eight or so young people milling around two tables at the far end of the food court, I saw Lisa pitch her jacket onto one of the benches. She walked up to one of the young men, threw her forearm across his shoulder and leaned into him. He appeared younger than she did, still in his teens. Putting an arm around her, his hand came to rest on her buttock well below the swag of a gold chain over her tight-fitting, wheat-colored tank top.

Standing shoulder high to him, she twitched in knee-high black leather boots, reached up for his cigarette, drew, exhaled the smoke and poked it back into his mouth.

For a moment, she looked back at Patrick in a somewhat plaintive mood, I thought. Was there too much disappointment in her life? Did she need, yearn, and hope?

About this time, her young buck spied Patrick, and pushing away from Lisa, met him with a high five. "Hey, my man." He squatted down to unzip the child's multi-colored jacket. Holding the coat in one hand, the fellow removed Patrick's red pull-on cap, leaving his friction-bothered blond strands standing on end. "Looks like you got new sneakers, there."

"Yeah." Patrick smiled up at him, put his arm around what's-his-face's neck and moved between his squatting legs. "Hey, want to go play *Mortal Combat* at the video arcade, huh?"

The young man rose up and stepped around Patrick. Tucking small gloves into the jacket pocket, he tossed it on top of Lisa's wrap. "Can't, Buddy, some other time." He allowed the child to fall away, untouched, before returning to the group around the table.

Listening to this play out, I needed to get closer to Patrick. Anyway, I suffered from the malodor of an over-flowing plastic waste bin nearby. Patrick begged a Slinky from one of Lisa's friends and played with it at the only unused table near his mother. "May I sit here with you? I'm Peg. What's your name?"

"Patrick."

"Well, Patrick, is your mom getting food while you hold down the table?"

"No-o," he said as though it were a stupid question. Without looking up from the Slinky, he pointed, "She's over there."

I whispered at him that I needed to speak to his mother, which he largely ignored.

With reporter's pad in hand, I touched Lisa lightly on the shoulder and she turned to me. "Forgive my intrusion, but Patrick," I pointed, "says you're his mother. I did not see an empty table and asked if I could sit with him while collecting my thoughts for a newspaper story. I don't want to cause you undue alarm on seeing a stranger with him."

Peering through large brown eyes, she said "Okay," and dismissed me with a flare of her hand. Her ringed fingers returned to a large dark, misshapen mole just beneath her left jaw.

I found her pretty, but thought her effectual ways with her man took cream from the top.

Back at the table, I took up mostly a one-sided conversation with Patrick, expressing things I thought a six-year-old might find interesting. "What about the green and gold leaves, and giant snowflakes hanging from the ceiling? Says snow for Santa's sleigh, doesn't it? The Christmas carols coming over the speakers put me in a gay mood. Do you like the words—"

"There ain't no Santa Claus!" he declared out of the blue.

That cut any chances of engaging him about Christmas, but I kept trying. Then Patrick opened a floodgate. He hated first grade, his teacher, and he had only two friends. "Kids at school don't like me. My teacher says I'm bad, and my mom don't like me neither. She says I'm dumb."

"But you're not, are you?"

"Nope." The Slinky flipped back and forth. Ker chink, ker chink. "You know what? I'm getting a bike for my birthday." Was it his first bike? Impatient with me, he said he had ridden a bike since he was three. "Spud took the training wheels off when I was four."

I asked if Spud was his friend.

"Nope, he's Mom's friend. You know what? He wouldn't go to the arcade with me."

Not easy to handle this kid, I thought with a yawn, realizing it was going on to eight o'clock. Patrick had not eaten and I was tired.

About that time, Lisa appeared at the table. Her friends were no longer on the scene. Flopping onto the seat across from me, she said she had a neighbor who worked at the paper. "Megan, that's her name. I don't think she knows that I live in the same townhouse complex. I have seen her coming and going, and in the park. I'm Lisa. What kind of story are you doing?"

"I'm Peg. Yes, I know Megan. What a small world." I explained I wanted to talk to working mothers raising children as single parents, as if it had nothing to do with her. "Do you know anyone who fits that category?"

She said she ought to since she was one, and gave several names of women who might participate. As I wrote her information, she agreed to an interview at her place on Sunday before she left for work. We set the hour, and she and Patrick ambled toward one of the food stalls.

The next day, I arrived at the appointed hour and heard her yell over the TV for Patrick to get the door. He swung it open without an invitation to enter, responding to my hello or missing a beat of the *Rambo* characters fighting, shooting and falling all over the screen.

Lisa ran water at the sink, slapped dishes onto the drain, and yelled, "Turn that damn noise off and go find those boys. Do something, but don't go to the park." To me, she voiced "Kids!" in an exasperated way. Drying her hands, she invited me to sit at the kitchen table.

Patrick hesitated with the remote, and his mother snatched it from his hands and swatted him on the backside. He defied her by taking his good time to grab a handful of Power Rangers before banging the door on his way out.

On the table, a half-eaten bowl of Spaghetti-O's® permeated the close room with the tang of tomatoes. Lacking an appreciation for tomatoes, the odor helped push the interview along.

Within the next hour, I learned a great deal about Lisa, who all the while played with the dark mole on her neck as though it were a security blanket.

The only girl and oldest of four siblings, she was born on an Air Force base in 1975. Nine years old when her family returned from a two-year assignment in Pakistan, Lisa left that country with images that bothered an impressionable child. She told of a holy man living on a bridge over the port waters. He wore a tattered loincloth—when he bothered to wear clothing at all—and slept on it at other times. His long, shaggy hair and beard were unkempt, and body un-bathed, but those who considered him a guru nourished him.

From guru to beggars, some came to the compound gate of Lisa's home. In some cases, they showed mouths with missing tongues cut out during the Pakistani-Indian upheaval. Such left her with nightmares. She and her mother met a beggar on a Karachi street. He had picked flesh from his arm down to the bone. "'Buckshee, Memsahib,' he said to my mother, holding his arm for us to see. Everyone just passed him by as if they didn't see him. I looked, and I wanted to puke."

Back in the states and living in Florida, Lisa was fourteen when she parted from her first boyfriend. The family moved to Virginia, and her father retired from the military to become a government service worker. "I was devastated, but that's the way the cookies crumble, I guess. You see this mole?" She pointed to her neck. "My Florida boyfriend thought it was ugly."

Once she began her story, I had to ask few questions.

She related that her mother came from a religious background. Forced Lisa and her brothers to church every Sunday and anytime the doors opened. "Always busy at the church." Lisa threw up her hand as if finished painting her mother. Then, laughing, she told of giving birth to Patrick at age sixteen. "After I found someone to replace the boy who didn't like my mole. I didn't know my 'newbie' long before I was pregnant."

She revealed these things to me, a stranger, without any hint of embarrassment.

Her dad wanted her to leave the home, "find her own way," but her mother had her way. Lisa went to a home for unwed mothers. Both parents wanted her to give up the baby for adoption, else find a way to support the child. "So, I've been supporting ever since," she said.

Her either-or-situation stitched my mind with pain. I could not imagine presenting my daughter with that choice, and reminded myself it was never my circumstance. Anyway, I must stick with facts and not get emotionally involved. Yet, I wondered if my children knew I loved them.

The provoking thought brought a pause in the questioning. I did not plan the interview technique of bothersome silence meant to push an interviewee to speak and reveal, but it worked.

"I don't know why I didn't give him up for adoption," Lisa continued. "I don't even like kids. They bother me."

She is honest, I thought, and dived into the core reason for being with her. She related that she did not handle the stresses of single, working motherhood well.

She rose, signaling the end of our time. I envied her shapely thighs shown off in tight blue jeans. Beyond envy, I wanted to take this waif of a girl in my arms, hold her and tell her she was loved. Tell her for all the times I had not said it to my children.

I did not give her a hug. Instead, I gave her a date when to expect the story to run in the newspaper.

We said goodbye, and Lisa called behind me that Patrick's birthday was just before Christmas. "He thinks he is getting a new bike, but I don't know."

I smiled back at her and drove home thinking of how to construct a story of her sad life.

My story about single working mothers was still unfinished two days after the interview. I switched on the TV news and dressed in a rush for work when I heard, ". . . the seven-year-old will be charged with attempted murder in the brutal beating of a four-week-old baby, whom doctors say is apt to have permanent brain damage."

Glancing up I gasped to see Lisa being led away, sobbing.

The reporter continued. "Two boys, who entered the apartment with the seven-year-old, are also charged with a misdemeanor for stealing a bicycle. According to police, the boys tearfully described the assault. The children's mothers told the media they didn't know why their sons did it."

Months later Patrick stood before a juvenile judge. When asked why he had beaten the baby, he said, "I don't know why I did it. I just wanted the bicycle."

I sat on the end of my bed, knowing this sad development put a whole other face on my list of story priorities. The single moms' feature would move below covering Patrick's trial and another feature idea—an investigative look at what becomes of very young children who spend time in juvenile detention. I thought about starting out twenty years earlier as a young reporter with visions of writing about the exploits of people like Amelia Earhart, war heroes, astronauts, and visionary people who made our nation great. I felt a longing for that simpler time, but reminded myself that the world has a way of rolling along, and we must deal with the present.

SOLVING AN
OLD MURDER CASE

I TURNED OFF THE TV, PICKED up the phone and dialed. "Chessie, did you see the news? Captain Wallace was just on television."

"What did he say, Jason? Have they caught the murderer?"

"Guess." I strung her along. "You'll never guess who—"

"It was Howard, the brother who never had any money. No, no, it had to be the butler. It's always the person you least suspect." Sounding more sure of her conclusion than I had felt, Chessie's level of excitement increased over the phone.

There was a long pause, as if she wanted to hear what I thought about her conclusion, and then I told her the real answer.

"Wow. Holy wow. I sort of thought that all along."

Two weeks ago I did not know, when our involvement began in the unsolved case, that it would be a big boon for me. When I was twelve, some of my classmates had called me nerdy because I said I wanted to be a crime reporter. But Chessie didn't call me a nerd. She said it did not matter because we were moving into high school and they probably would not be in our classes.

She is so smart, and the reason I am writing this crime report just the way it happened.

Our adventure began in the cemetery. On school days, Chessie and I walked through St. Mary's Cemetery on our way to and from Alexandria

Junior High. The resting places with their moss-covered headstones and weathered tomb covers, seemingly as old as time, drew us in to explore during our summer break.

Several weeks ago, we huddled in a vaulted tomb, wondering what to do now that we were inside it. "Where's the flashlight?" Chessie's raspy whisper had echoed in the hallowed, hollow space. "Hurry, Jason. Gads, why did you take up my dare? My heart's pounding like a drum."

I told her to keep her socks on, that I had the light. I did not admit to her, but my heart beat like ready to jump through my skin too. Except for a sliver of sun slipping through a small opening in the heavy vault door and pasting itself on the back wall, we were in almost total darkness. I pulled the small flashlight from my jeans pocket and shined it up and down the rows of interments.

"What . . . Jason, shine the light up here." Chessie clung to my arm as I held the light beam on what appeared to be something stuffed into a crevice between two entombment chambers. Working it loose with her fingers, she unfolded the white velvet wrapping.

We crouched on the floor, transfixed by the brilliant mounted gemstone held on the palm of her hand. Stunned speechless, my hands shook, and she told me to hold the flashlight still. Time slipped by as we hunched down, gaping at the stone.

Then, Chessie slipped the ring on her long slender finger, and my sweetheart's pretty face danced before my eyes. I gulped, thinking about the things we planned after college. I am not going to put this part in my report.

Regaining a voice, I said it must be worth ka-zillions. "We must take it to the police."

She stood, folded the wrapping around her find, and looked at me with big blue questioning eyes. "You think?" She pointed to my pocket, "Yours or mine?" I indicated hers, and Chessie pulled up her tee-top to jam the gem down into her jeans. I grabbed her hand, and we pushed the heavy vault door closed before racing to the police station.

At the station house, the captain took the wrapped ring with the huge stone and led us into a small room. Pointing, he instructed, "Sit there, kids." After telling him where we found the treasure, he said it was the Helms solitaire diamond, missing since the murder of Cynthia Helms in 1985. "The case is still open. Her assailant is still at large," he added.

The murder happened before our time, so the captain filled us in on the details.

He said a house servant found Mrs. Helms' bludgeoned body when she took a breakfast tray into the woman's bedroom. Her scream brought the butler on a run. He called the police and the murdered woman's two sons. Later, he called her elderly brother, Howard, a destitute bum. "Some said Mrs. Helms was rather fond of Howard Meakins, and on a regular basis, she shoveled money his way. Unknown to her, he gambled or spent it on women.

"Right away, the police hauled Howard in," the captain said, "but no evidence was ever found to pinpoint him as the murderer. Anyway, some woman gave him an alibi. A murder weapon is yet to be found. No fingerprints, nothing." He said whoever committed the crime left the scene clean. "The coroner said a blunt instrument was used, and the butler claimed a tall brass candlestick was missing from Mrs. Helms' room."

Captain Wallace remembered questioning all the family members, including Mrs. Helms' sons, Kevin and Lester. All were ruled out as suspects when her will revealed the diamond was to be auctioned at her death and proceeds from the estate divided between the two sons. "Anyway," he said, "her sons—wealthy in their own rights—and their wives and kids had alibis for the time of the murder."

The butler, a faithful employee for twenty years, did not have a scintilla of suspicion pointed at him, but Mrs. Helms had often accused someone of taking jewelry from her dresser. According to Howard Meakins, his wealthy sister accused one of the servants of stealing her jewelry.

"Juanita Belks—that's the servant who found the body—well, she wept and admitted Mrs. Helms accused her of stealing a diamond broach. Juanita claimed she found it in a clothing drawer where the dear lady hid it."

Captain Wallace dropped the paperclip he had been turning end over end, picked up the wrapped diamond and leaned back in his chair. "Well, kids, you may have brought the evidence we need to solve this mystery." He said the vault and diamond might hold fingerprints, and the wrapping after a thorough scanning might reveal forensic evidence such as hair. "We didn't have all the modern tools, DNA, stuff like that, back in 1985. DNA evidence was not trusted by the courts anyway. All the possible suspects will be brought in again." He paused, running a hand over his gray hair. "Family members are always highly suspect in cases where inheritance is involved," he said, "but it's hard to believe any one of them had a motive."

Chessie and I stood, knowing it was time to leave the treasure in the hands of the police.

At this point, my report ended for the time being. I did not intend to let Chessie read it before it was finished. Meantime, the newspapers and television carried stories about us finding the diamond. Since I intend to be a police reporter, I followed all the progress in the case. Whom did they question? What evidence did they find?

Over the weeks, Chessie kept asking, "Who do you think murdered Mrs. Helms?"

Then today, I turned on the television news, and there was Captain Wallace before a deck of reporters' microphones. "We have the alleged murderer. I am going to turn the mike over to Prosecuting Attorney Mark Myles. He will answer some of your questions."

I stood watching the TV as the lawyer stepped to the microphone, and in response to one question said, "Yes, we think we have substantial evidence to bring charges and a trial soon."

"Can you give us a name?" an unseen reporter yelled out.

Captain stepped forward. "Well, we have two people in custody."

All at one time, a barrage of questions stormed from the media, but one asked, "Who are the persons and what links them to the crime?"

Captain Wallace hesitated, then, he said DNA matter linked the victim's sons to the wrapping around the recovered diamond. "We must determine which son. The other suspect is one of Mrs. Helms' maids, and we think we can make that determination by questioning her." The captain waited for the reporters' speaking over each other to quiet. "Well, I would compromise the case if I answered those questions. Wait for those accused to be tried in a trial." He held up his hand. "Ladies and gentlemen, that's it. All the evidence we have will need to be proven in court."

His dismissal of the news gatherers caused a rush of noise. The TV camera showed Captain Wallace reentering the police station, and that was when I called Chessie.

Several days after the accused received sentences of years in prison, my boon came when the phone rang, and Captain Wallace said, "Jason, can you and Chessie come down to my office right away?"

"Gosh, Captain Wallace, did we do something wrong?"

"You'll find out when you get here."

Shaking in my boots, I called Chessie. After calming her down, we hurried downtown.

The captain seated us in his office and said we helped solve the Helms murder case.

He said Lester Helms denied any part in his mother's murder, claiming one of the servants, Bridgett Estes, did it. "Lester said he found her wearing stolen jewelry. We brought Miss Estes in, told her what Helms claimed. She went into a tirade, calling him a traitor among a few other choice names. But it was your help that led us to them." The captain grinned.

"Why would she call him a traitor? And what evidence showed that Lester had something to do with his mother's murder?"

"Well, Jason, Miss Estes claimed Lester encouraged her to steal his mother's jewelry. He allowed her to keep less valuable pieces, and we located evidence from shops where he sold the more expensive gems. DNA showed that Lester hid the diamond in the crypt. Bridgett claimed they engaged in an illicit affair of many years, right up until arrested. She said Lester had her steal the diamond and helped her kill his mother before they were to flee to France. Apparently, he did not intend to take Bridgett to France. He convinced her that selling the diamond was too risky. It would lead to their arrest and imprisonment."

"But how long was it in the crypt and what was he going to do with it?" Chessie asked.

The captain leaned back in his chair and smiled at her. Lester owned up to hiding it there soon after his mother's interment, safe for such a time that he may need it. "Well, Kids, because you helped us solve the case, I want to arrange an awards ceremony and present you on the television. What do you think?"

"Whew, Captain Wallace, we thought we . . . well, gee whiz, we'd like that, wouldn't we Chessie?" Still a little pale from the call to the station, she nodded.

"Jason, Chessie, this is what happens when you cooperate with the law." Captain Wallace stood, walked behind us and patted our shoulders, saying he would set up a ceremony date.

On the way home, I told Chessie about my report. "Now, I can write the end to it. Would you like to read it?"

She gave me an enthusiastic "yes," and we felt proud for doing the right thing.

CLAY FOR MOLDING IMOGENE

A BREEZE PLAYED WITH WHITE PRISCILLA curtains at the open bedroom window, the sole comfort reaching out to the dry-eyed mother. Imogene rocked in a gentle, thoughtful way in a high-backed chair. Her only daughter lay in a dove gray coffin trimmed in mauve pink in the Hammond Funeral Chapel, awaiting burial services the next day. Imogene had cried all the tears she could cry. Now, she needed to sort it all out.

LouEllen was too young to die. Imogene could not let go of that reality. A broken record played in her head. Did I love her? Did you know I loved you, LouEllen? "Oh, God," she muttered and made a shallow sigh.

Downstairs, friends and relatives came and went, offering condolences to Sam and Pete. Imogene left protocol to her husband, son and grandchildren. Sam could weather the loss of his stepdaughter. His relationship with LouEllen had always been tenable, to say the least. He could never feel the hurt and doubts she was feeling.

Pete, seven years younger than his half-sister, never seemed to have close feelings for her. He lived on the California coast and LouEllen nearby in northern Virginia. They had so little in common. They did not even write to each other. Their mother wiped a single tear oozing down her cheek.

Imogene did not notice that spring moved over the landscape in a bright balmy glow. The outside clime all of a sudden sent a stronger breeze through the window. She paid it no heed even though it whipped a wisp of gray hair across her forehead. Pushing strands back in place in a blank-headed manner, she remembered telling Sam not to disturb her.

Rocking in a rhythmic manner for a time she could not tell, her mind finally wandered away from love-guilt for LouEllen.

How different it was when Papa and Mama died. "Mama, I don't think you loved me." Her lips moved but no discernible words formed. She felt her papa did not love his family; else, he would not have left. Why did he leave? Why?

Her blank gaze saw nothing more than images from her past. Her face had once smitten a number of beaus. Now it sagged in loose folds of aging dullness. Wrinkles were her enemies. They sneaked up on her over the years and went unrecognized until her second marriage did not bring the anticipated happiness she expected. Sam, a devout man, brought out a deep guilt in her when she miscarried their first child. She questioned her self-worth, and to this day, still did.

When they married, she was young, happy and naive. Had happiness eluded her? LouEllen had said that she lived her life as though happiness had eluded her. Imogene had a need to know, to review. "Mama, did you love me?" she demanded, pounding the chair arms with clinched fists.

Footsteps approaching up the stairs quelled her pounding. She did not remember locking the door. Turning toward it, she waited, expecting it to open and thinking she would not go downstairs, no matter who it was. *Why can't they let me be for a while?*

The door flew open, and Pete stomped into the room. "Are you all right? We heard thumps up here. What were you doing?" He stood over her with a commanding, accusatory face that said she was committing another wrong.

"Go away." Imogene's words surprised her. Always the meek one, she cowed before her husband and children. She did not even try to answer his questions but looked at her son as though he were a stranger.

"Ah, Ma, come downstairs. People are asking for you. We don't know what to tell them."

"Go away, Pete."

He turned and was almost through the door, and she said, "Tell them Imogene will be down when she's ready. Tell them I have wrinkles to iron out. Tell them whatever you wish."

Her son looked at his mother as though she were someone he had met for the first time. He shook his head in apparent disbelief and headed for the stairway.

Imogene sat alone again, hardly believing she had taken command of the situation. She felt strong but did not understand where the strength came from. Then, she thought of Sam, her husband, and fear reigned along with disgust. She knew he would bound up the stairs as soon as Pete told him how she had acted. How could she defend herself from his harsh words?

He will say, "How come you're acting like a smart aleck, Imogene?" That is what he will say. He will tell me to brace up and get your smartness down those stairs. Why should I have to listen to all those people coming in here acting as if they were crazy about your daughter and mouthing sympathy for you? That is what he will say. What am I going to do? Wondering, she looked around as if to find somewhere to hide.

Before she could decide, Sam came through the door Pete had left open. "Enough is enough, Imogene. Get up and get downstairs. She was your daughter, not mine." He walked around the chair and stood squarely in front of her, a commanding presence. "Well, are you gonna get up or am I going to get you out of that chair?"

Imogene looked up at him, and relishing the earlier moments with Pete, Sam did not seem so overpowering. She stared at him without moving and in disbelief of her own self-control. For some reason his words did not intimidate her as they always had. She motioned to another chair and said, "Sit down, Sam."

Appearing taken aback, Sam stuttered something she could not understand, but he took the few steps to the chair, turned and glanced back at her.

She noted the question in his expression. It was all too new to her. "Sit," she said. It was not an invitation, more of an order.

Sam eased down onto the chair, and Imogene felt energized, alive.

"No, Sam. LouEllen wasn't your daughter. Any fool would know you never considered her as yours." Imogene paused, waiting to know what to say next. "I've been sitting here questioning my own love for her. Was I a loving mother?" she asked. "Maybe any mother who loses a child is fearful that she hasn't shown enough love. She knows it's too late and realizes she will never be able to show how deep her love really was."

Sam shifted on the chair as though uncomfortable with this whole display of concern, but he uttered not a sound. He sat, rubbing together calloused, Kansas-weathered hands. Long ago farm work left him rough cut.

Imogene was not going to let this moment escape her, and she plowed on. "Well, I think LouEllen knew I loved her. I did, you know. All these years, I have allowed others to treat me like a dormouse. Was too quick to agree, or say, 'Oh no, I do not mind doing it. Well, I'm tired, Sam."

No longer fearing him, she waited for him to speak.

Sam seemed unable to pull up words from his well of plenty.

Imogene began rocking. In a few minutes, she spoke into the silence. "I've found the clay to mold a new me. Don't ask where it came from. All I know is that I began to examine and found myself lacking."

Moments ticked by. Neither spoke, but Sam appeared to be considering. Then, he smiled that grin, the one that had attracted her many years ago. "Atta girl. Give her some spunk. I'm going to like my new Imogene." He gave her a peck on the cheek. "Come down when you're ready," he said from the door.

Imogene sat for a few minutes, digesting what had taken place. Then, she stood, pulled the frumpy dress over her head, and went to her closet. Standing there, she held the selected better wear pants suit and wondered if it took the death of her only daughter to make her a whole person. Dressing in front of the full-length mirror, careful for her looks, she muttered, "Well, LouEllen, maybe happiness hasn't eluded me altogether."

She gave her hair a few brush strokes and made a last survey of herself in the mirror. Standing tall, Imogene pulled her shoulders back and started for the stairs.

NIGHTMARE

A BLOWING COLD FEBRUARY EVENING DID not keep us from our prestigious host's repast. Noted for his dinner parties—fit for the palate with conversational food fit for thought—Dr. Hamlin was a distinguished professor emeritus at George Washington University.

Some of his guests were better known than Dr. Hamlin. Others were not. During the course of the evening, balding government heads flirted with young things. World War II vets leaned into fading wives, and tired press members hounded tablemates. Some of the gathered were former hippies-gone-yuppies and their yuppettes. I was the only Arkansan in the mix.

Mixed was the way His Honor liked it, sparking fires of dissension in which one could only agree to disagree. Dr. Hamlin believed that agreeing to disagree was the way man could save himself and his world.

After dinner, we moved into the parlor, there to delve deeper and deeper into world problems and leap all over global happenings.

Dr. Hamlin filled up his overstuffed leather chair. He sat scrunched down with feet on a matching ottoman. His eyeglasses rested on his nose, and except for a short thin fluff of hair on his head, he could almost be mistaken for Benjamin Franklin.

The only guest without a partner, I sat in the Victorian style lady's chair and wondered why I was invited. Our host did not have a mate, and I guessed as a duo, we rounded out his dinner table with an even number. My media friends caught my attention with individual brags about their headline-grabbing stories. All four slouched on a couch. Two argued over which newspaper or television network got the scoop. Veterans fell into battle tales while their salon-coiffed wives smiled and remained unengaged. As for the yuppies, they talked finances, offered cures for the government and tips for working the stock market.

Dr. Hamlin filled his pipe, lit it, and listened to talk around the room for a few minutes until a lull gave him the chance to quiet the chatter and hang out a new topic for discussion. It might be controversial, or not.

We grazed in religious pastures from Genesis through the Renaissance and the Twentieth Century, making philosophical comparisons and exploring states of consciousness. We abided for a while in a book, *The Satanic Verses*, written by an Asian Indian-Brit sentenced to death by the Ayatollah of Iran for blaspheming Islam. Then as though to escape thoughts of Salman Rushdie's dilemma, someone suggested a round robin of story telling.

The old English professor blew pipe smoke toward the ceiling. "Let's make it voluntary and limit the genre to fiction or creative non-fiction anecdotes. Agreed?"

When it came my turn, I told about the Preacher Man.

"Forty years ago," I began, "an August evening in southwest Arkansas held onto the heat as if it were a treasured condition, but the Preacher Man came to convince otherwise."

I planted my scene of the makeshift outdoor setting between village stores with rows of long raw plank benches facing a gravel highway and filled with women and youngsters. I explained how Jimmy Hickok and the rest of us barely teenagers netted out mothers' reprimands for making a mockery of Miss Elsie Waylock and the preacher.

My story stirred giggles and an uproar of laughter and hand clapping at its end.

Perhaps it was my story that set off the weirdest dream I think I shall ever experience. With soundness of sleep had come this hellish little figure. This HE THING . . . an ugly little bastard sat there in my dream, reading my Sunday comics in my overstuffed chair. He was so minuscule that no one else could see him. Not that anyone else was there to see him.

Crossing spidery little legs, he bobbed one hairy foot to the beat of a metronome.

My feet froze in place. I could not run, and my heart beat with the sound of a dove taking flight. What could I do but stand there listening to the darnedest story I had ever heard?

"God is the Great I Am," he said. "Everything. Male, female, black and white, like the chameleon, takes on whatever color it needs. Good and bad, me and you, Christian, Moslem, Jew, Hindu, Buddhist . . . birds and beasts, the fish and fowl, fire and air and earth and stone . . . the Am, man! The goo holding it all together in a universal womb, sealed with a boom."

"You little cuss," I screamed. "I wish I had a name for you, you smell like semen. Maybe it's blood! You foul, repulsive creature, I hate your guts! You contradict everything I know about God."

He had my attention. I whipped out my Bible and quoted, and questioned, and he got me every time, as his reedy, broken record-like voice grooved my brain. I hated him, and yet, there was a strong attraction. A love affair with the devil, I told myself, shouting blasphemies.

I awoke from the nightmare thinking Hell had a hold on me. I lay there, puzzling. Was it punishment for past and present misdeeds? What did it all mean? Maybe I ought to review my training and consider the use of my pen. Stick to the facts when writing about politicians and others.

With these thoughts in mind, it dawned on me that I had a new story to share if invited to another Dr. Hamlin party.

A SENSE OF PLACE

*P*ULLING THE KAYAK INTO THE cove, I soon tied up at the dock and sat there listening to the quiet lapping of waves and letting the memories flow.

Across a span of green, the house stood out on an unattended lawn. Wraparound porches managed to weather the worst of the nor'easters storming across New England. A single white clapboard sagged toward the porch from the otherwise intact siding. Warm morning sun struck the upstairs windows and bent the light back at me.

Mother's voice flooded across my mind, scolding my sister for strewing her wraps and shoes about, and me for leaving toys on the stairway. Mother was a dear while a stickler for neatness. The chandelier prisms catching the light over the dining room table came clearly to mind. And Nora, Mother's housekeeper of many years, working her feather duster.

In the evening, Dad sat in his leather chair reading the Boston Globe while old Chester, our golden retriever, snored nearby. Chester's blond hair grayed around his ears and paws. Occasionally he grunted and stretched. He gave those long and short snorts as though difficult for him to breathe. It was, but he was faithful to the end.

We buried our beloved dog in a back corner of the lawn and put up a makeshift memorial to him. I must check if it is still there.

I stood and stepped up onto the dock.

Walking up the knoll toward the Norway spruce, I remembered the classical combo music and gay laughter coming from the large white tent during my sister's wedding reception. Her name is Abigail. Abby to us, she is six years older than I. What year was Abby married? I was sixteen. 1988? Was it that long ago? Abby and Arne live in Florida now. My nieces and nephew are grown and in college.

I had many a romp on this lawn with Norman and Jeff. Who were the other guys that came and went? Have I forgotten their names? Eric. We were a rough bunch, playing touch football, lawn croquet, and whatever we could do to cause mischief. Ah, Kevin, our leader. Man, did we get in trouble when caught with six packs of Coors in the boathouse. Every parent on this side of Mackinaw Pond was on my parents' case. Wonder where they are. What course did they take?

I stepped out of the kayak and walked to the back of the house. Part of old Chester's marker remained upright. The horizontal arm of the cross lay on the ground. "Hello, old boy. I will repair your place when I return."

I made a tour inside the house. It required a good cleaning, painting and upgrading of appliances. Upstairs and downstairs, plus modernizing the baths. I felt relieved that Ellen had not come with me. She would not be happy with what she saw.

I locked the front door and sat down on the wide stack of porch steps.

Look at that pond, calm as the summer's breeze. What a time we had . . . boating, fishing, water ski-ing. I met Christine that summer. I sat on the boat dock, my eyes riveted on that graceful form with long dark hair flagging the air as she skimmed behind the boat. Making a wide swing, the boat brought her close to the dock and she waved. I felt I had swallowed my heart. She was so stunningly gorgeous in a bikini.

Where is she now? Beautiful Christine. She sure stirred up the old male hormones. Yep, we loved each other. Would be married now had I not gone off to Silicon Valley after college.

"Please don't go, my love," she had said. "I'm a New England girl, Chad. I cannot imagine living on the West Coast. I think I would be miserable, and misery can lead to divorce."

She broke my heart, and I think hers too. Yeah, if . . .

Suddenly, reality struck. A divorcee with graying temples and the beginning of a middle age paunch, I left a well-paying position as a senior softwear engineer to take a lesser paying engineering job. Just to come here to live.

Ellen complained about living on less pay. One failed marriage and here I am about to be hitched to Ellen.

Whoa! Am I having second thoughts? Come to think, I was not all that crazy about living in California. So, why am I taking another wife from there? What if this cold climate . . . ? It is a place where the sun does not shine every day. It will make Ellen miserable.

Yep, Ellen will be living here, in the house I inherited when Dad died. My sister does not want any part of it, but I love this place on the pond. It is the place of so many memories—where I met Christine. Just the thought of Christie sent me into a spiral.

I have to find Christine.

WILLOW CREEK HONKY TONK

*L*AST EVENING, MARGARET ANNE SAT in the living room when her father came to his easy chair. He picked up the newspaper, grunted, and placed it on his lap. "Maggie," he said, "Judge Austin's boy is as wild as a March hare!"

Maggie Anne moved to the arm of her father's chair, leaned close and reached her arm across his shoulder. "Oh, Daddy, I know Joel is a bit wild, but every girl in this town wants to be his girlfriend. Name one other girl who can ride around in a fancy car with a college fellah."

He looked up into her face, and she returned as much adoration as her eyes could hold. "Don't worry, Daddy, I know how to handle Joel Austin."

George Brice had given his Maggie the clue to his heart on her seventeenth birthday. He told his only child that she had her mother's zest for life. "Her liveliness attracted me to my Mary. Frightened me too," he had said, adding Maggie had inherited her mother's beautiful red hair and a resolute stubbornness from him. "That's a cause for concern." Laughing, he had given his daughter a birthday hug.

She knew her daddy disliked Joel's father. Attorney Brice knew about Judge Austin's accrued land deals. How he increased his bottom acreage near the Achoochee River when bank foreclosures came due and loan payments were not met. "He garnered up the land of farmers. That old man can well afford the sporty new Cabriolet he sent that boy off to the university in." George had questioned the lasting value of the judge's holdings since the '29 crash, saying the new president seemed committed to taking drastic steps against the depressed times.

45

Then yesterday in the sewing room, before the conversation with her father, Maggie's mother had set the sewing machine on fast stitching. She sewed together a white dotted Swiss dress with a tie-in-front red sash for her daughter's first date with Joel. Maggie stood on a dining chair. "Mid-calf, Mother, the hemline is at the calf of my leg." She had watched her mother walk around the chair with a mouthful of pins, folding and pinning the hem.

With the last pin in place, Mary had looked up at her daughter. "Maggie, he's the town's handsomest and most eligible boy. It makes me feel almost young again. My young Irish heart leapt at fun, but in this small town . . . and there is your daddy's position too. Being he's a lawyer and all." Pushing back a strand of fading hair, she had given her daughter a wistful look. "Your daddy will be worried, Maggie Anne. He had it easy with me . . . always subdued and submissive when what I wanted . . . Oh, never mind, dear. You're coming of age in a different time."

Her mother had hugged her when she stepped down from the chair. "Your father knows when he's lost a case," she had said. "Have fun, Maggie dear, but remember he'll worry."

From the living room, Maggie and her mother had heard the arch-shaped, table-model radio come alive with the voice of H. V. Kaltenborn. "Evening, folks. We-ell, it looks like . . ."

"Shush in there!" her father had insisted, when their sewing room voices reached him.

Mary had whispered that she should not worry for her dress would be hemmed in time.

Now, Maggie Anne stood before a full-length mirror in her bedroom, puffing the sleeves and admiring her new dress. She liked the way the red sash pulled in her waist, showing off her curves. In minutes, Joel would ring the doorbell.

She smiled, thinking of the beguiling way she had teased and cajoled her father to win him over yet again.

Joel spirited her out the front door before her daddy demanded a time to have her home.

Driving to the Bijou Theater, Joel said he had spent the day with his father, watching farm hands plow under acres of the healthiest cotton plants along the river. "Daddy spit on that fresh plowed ground and said 'Damn Roosevelt! No telling what that so-and-so will have us doing next.'"

He said he knew the townsfolk did not care much for his father, but he did not feel he had to justify him. "Daddy is just Daddy. It's envy, anyway."

Maggie made a mental note not to mention any of this to her father. She watched Joel's profile and thought his mind had gone far away. Then he turned a handsome face her way and said he would not be returning to the university in the fall.

At the theater, Mae West starring in *She Done Him Wrong* soon blurred Maggie's sufferings from stifling heat, and the smell of sweat and saccharine talcum powder.

After the movie, she and Joel stayed for the Bank Night drawing. The announcer gave the name of a lucky winner before the late movie began and the early Saturday night crowd poured out of the theater into an empty street.

In the summer night air, Joel guided the car from the curb and headed for the edge of town.

As the car sped along, Maggie Anne laid her head back against the black leather seat, closed her eyes, and let the breeze whip bobbed hair across her face.

Suddenly, Joel broke the silence. "Did I tell you I won't go back to school in September?"

"Yes, but why?" Maggie Anne questioned, but Joel offered nothing more. She was not too sad about that. He is so handsome, she thought, admiring him from a peripheral view. Mrs. Joel Justin III . . .

Thoughts of a prospective married name gave way to the "clunk, clunk, clunk" of the Willow Creek wooden bridge, jolting her back to reality. "What are we doing way out heah, Joel?"

"What's the matter? Don't tell me you're afraid of the woods, Maggie." He threw back his head and laughed at his tease. "Want to go dancing, girl?" he asked, pulling the car to a stop close to the ditch across from Willow Creek Honky Tonk.

Maggie Anne smoothed short waves away from her face and peered across at the place she had only heard about. Brother Powell had called it a "den of iniquity!" in a Sunday sermon. "Daddy will kill me," she murmured.

"You're daddy doesn't have to know. Are you coming, Maggie?" Joel challenged her with a devilish grin, leaving her with a yen to tousle his dark well-groomed hair, greased to a shine.

Suddenly, she heard strands of Kate Smith's *When the Moon Comes Over the Mountain* spinning out on the Victrola record. Nature took up the chorus in the still night. From deep in the woods, a band of crickets chirped without a break in their performance. Down along Willow Creek, hoarse frogs croaked for rain.

A sickening sweet scent of honeysuckle, growing along the ditch, nudged Maggie's nose skyward to avoid the repugnant smell she abhorred. Then, through an opening in the trees, she caught the stars winking in a flirtatious way, daring her. Strains of a Latin rumba set up a rhythmic twitch in her body. Ready to hit the dance floor, she asked, "Why shouldn't we go dancing?" She felt as flippant as she sounded.

She slid across the seat, and Joel took her hand as she stepped from the running board.

Hand in hand, they walked toward the unpainted, rough-board building at the fork, where Willow Creek Bottom Road left off the main road between Fulmire and Ashton.

Tied back wooden shutters allowed patches of light to form on the ground beneath window openings. Maggie Anne tried to remember when Moss Braden began having Saturday night dances in the two-room structure thrown up as a religious meetinghouse before a church could be built at Shiloh. Taking ownership of the building behind the church people, Moss named his joint the Willow Creek Fish Camp. He divided the larger room into small cubicles containing long board tables and benches on which he served family-style, all-you-can-eat fried catfish, hush puppies, fried potatoes, sliced onions and pickles for fifty cents a head.

At some point, he turned the isolated place into a honky tonk. Even the sheriff knew that Moss' moonshine attracted men to the place. It was said that he transported it by Model-A truck from a well-hidden still located somewhere in the bottom woods behind Willow Creek.

Maggie and Joel entered the crowded room. It was alive with motion, and they joined other fox-trotters and two-steppers on the dance floor. The hand-cranked Victrola, from its place on a former fish-fare table, ground out *Three Little Words*.

They were into the Continental step, then the Carioca as the evening whirled by. All the while, Maggie took in the surroundings. Kerosene lanterns hung from wall nails. Overall-clad men made crude swearing, and made-up women sent peals of laughter across the room. Soft light spread over the smoke-filled room. Malodorous kerosene, sweat and Evening In Paris perfume caught Maggie's attention at various times.

She loved to dance even if Brother Powell deemed it sinful. She learned most of the steps from Miss Broughton, director of the high school Glee Club, who dreamed up song-and-dance routines for school play intermissions. She kept in practice with radio tunes, and her father did not seem to mind as long as she was not dancing with boys.

Joel proved to be a good partner, but now, he headed for the sideline, tugging Maggie by the hand. Finding a place for her on one of the benches along the wall, he excused himself and disappeared out the side door.

Not content to sit in a sweat among other wallflowers, Maggie moved to one of the back, open windows to catch a breath of air moved by large water oaks on the lawn. Soon she heard restless horses, hitched to wagons, stomp their impatient hooves. Then, through the window came, "Where is Moss?" That is Joel's voice, she thought. "Ya'll been passing that quart jar of corn liquor among yourselves? How about if I take a swig?"

There was laughter. "Hey there, Joel, have you been off to school, buddy?" More laughter, then, "That's a pretty gal you got in there, Joel."

About this time, Maggie Anne spotted Mr. Will Drews, one of the church deacons. He danced so close to the woman in a print dress . . . That is not Mrs. Drews. Good heavens! He will see me. She had to make a quick move.

Maggie walked over and tapped the man on the shoulder. "What time is it, Mr. Drews?"

He turned and, seeing Maggie Anne, stopped in mid-step. "Maggie Anne! Why, uh, well, it must be getting late." He stumbled away from the print-clad woman. Her approach seemed to have a sobering effect on him. Reeking of corn liquor, he walked off toward the wall bench.

Maggie followed him. "I won't mention I saw you here, Mr. Drews, if you don't tell a soul you saw me. Agreed?"

"Yes, yes, agreed." He mopped a stained handkerchief across his wrinkled brow and swiped his double chin.

Maggie Anne nodded her okay, and seeing Joel reenter the side door, she left Mr. Drews to meet him. He smelled like Moss' illegal potion too. "You've been drinking, Joel."

"I took just a few swigs to fortify myself. Help me forget about Daddy's ultimatum. It sounds like I'm destined to life on the farm, Maggie."

"It's late, Joel. My daddy will want to know where I have been. I must think of something. I know! We had a flat tire. And . . . and you had a devil of a time fixing it."

"Ah, Maggie, tell him Saturday nights are for drowning worries of the past week . . . and scratching out any thoughts of the ones coming up."

Maggie enjoyed dancing, but she did not relish lying to her father. He may be right about Joel Austin III, and she had second thoughts about him too.

SAD IS THE HEART

*O*CTOBER SUN CAST THE DAY bright, but inside the Miller house, a cloud lingered over Jeannie. For months rumors floated, and now the dreaded day had arrived.

Almost time to leave, she thought, letting the bedroom blind fall back in place. Let me send him away with a smile as bright as that sun. I will not cry today. Please do not let me cry. A single tear traced down her cheek. Wiping it away with her hand, Jeannie brushed back her long dark hair into a ponytail and picked up her handbag and a light wrap.

She tiptoed into the family room and stood behind Dan.

He sat on the couch with Danielle on one knee and Kevin on the other.

"Why are you going away, Daddy?" His five-year-old daughter fingered the camouflaged sleeve of his fatigues. Danielle turned a questioning face up to Dan, and Jeannie wiped the corner of her stole across her eyes. Her chubby two-year-old Kevin played with their father's beret.

Dan jiggled them on his knees, and Jeannie watched him struggle for words.

Then, lifting Danielle's chin, he said, "Look at me, sweetheart. Daddy's going . . ." Dan choked on his explanation. "I'm going to a far away land . . . b-because I love you so much. You must always remember that. It's because I love you, and Kevin, and Mommy so much. Will you do something for me? While I'm away, will you remind your brother that Daddy is away because he loves you?"

"Uh huh, I'll tell him all the time." Danielle reached her arms around his neck. "I love you too, Daddy."

51

"That's my girl."

Jeannie swallowed her own hurt. Wanting to soothe the pain heard in her husband's choked emotion, she bent, snuggled her face into his shoulder and kissed his neck.

Dan reached up and clasped her head, holding her in place for a moment. His voice under control, he told Danielle and Kevin to get their coats. "It's time to go to the base."

Jeannie stepped back into the bedroom and grabbed a handful of tissues. She must not let Dan see the mess she was making of this day. When she emerged from the room, he held a duffel bag in one hand and his cap in the other. All three waited at the door for her.

"Are we ready?" Jeannie tried on a bright face.

"We waited for you, Mommy." Danielle's face held a not-quite-understanding smile.

Jeannie picked up Kevin, caught her daughter's hand, and they walked out to the car.

On the drive to the National Guard armory, where the men would deploy, Jeannie pointed out fall colors on hillsides. "Look, kids. I wonder if old Jack Frost came through here with his paint buckets and spread all these trees in pretty bright colors." Her preschool student knew her primary colors, but Jeannie pointed anyway and asked, "What is that color, Danielle?"

She answered, "Red," and her mother added, "There are oranges, pinks, purples . . . and green too." She kept up the chatter about anything other than today's parting.

At the armory, time moved toward that ending. Other families and couples stood in groups, distancing themselves in the private moments left to them.

Dan knelt, one knee on the tarmac. He drew Danielle and Kevin to himself so that they could circle his neck with their small arms.

Jeannie waited through the long hard moment for her turn. She did not catch Dan's whispers to his children.

He took each by a hand and stood. "Danielle hold Kevin's hand and stand here by Mommy." He pulled Jeannie into his embrace and they clung to each other.

Then, it was time. A minute would have to last for six months, and that could turn into a year. She pulled back with a smile, hoping it was fit to melt her husband's heart.

"That's the face I want to remember." Dan pulled her close again. Then, releasing her, he picked up his duffel and walked toward the plane that would take him to Afghanistan—take him out of their lives. For how long Jeannie did not know.

Dan turned, waved, and disappeared into the bowels of the plane.

Month moved into month with Jeannie crossing them off on the calendar. She pulled out photo albums, showing Danielle and Kevin pictures of their daddy and talking about him. Somehow, she passed the lonely time across the span of days without giving in to feelings that pushed against her strength.

When friends stopped them on the street to ask about Dan, Danielle said, "My Daddy had to go away 'cause he loves us." She stayed faithful about reminding Kevin.

After many months, Dan's tour neared an end. A roadside bomb blew close to the truck in which he rode.

Following surgery to remove his left hand and half of the forearm, he recuperated in Walter Reed Hospital. Jeannie and the children visited him and discovered the forefinger on his right hand was also missing. Dan's pain was not all physical. He carried it in his square-jawed face and brown eyes.

Her husband would bear the burden of what he had witnessed, of a stump arm and missing finger. While Jeannie suffered his loss too, to her he was as whole as ever. Her heaviest burden lifted when her wholesome man came home.

SPARSE BOUNTY

*G*ARETH FINISHED A HEARTY BREAKFAST at Cap'n Jake's Crab House, paid his tab, exchanged a few words with Marge, the waitress, and headed down the marina pier. He guided his outboard motorboat into the Wicomico River, turned off the engine and paddled up-river with the oars.

The Wicomico flowed southeast into the Potomac River at Rock Point. Gareth revered Maryland's streams. Today, he planned to go about five miles inland, near to the river's headwaters. He intended to start the motor when he tired. Meantime, he meant to enjoy the sights and sounds.

The waterman and Nora his wife lived across Neal Sound on Cobb Island. A lifetime of labor on the water showed in Gareth's ruddy complexion. He worked year-round, often with Nora as his helpmate, but they planned to retire soon.

It would be hard to give up his trade. He found the Chesapeake Bay and its tributaries exhilarating, but climbing on and off his workboat and lifting tongs loaded with oysters became more difficult each day. Oyster season ran from September through April. Gareth crabbed for Maryland blues, and seined rockfish and bluefish from May through August. He had no sons to help and continue on the water after he retired. His fellow watermen also realized their offspring were not inclined to take up the hard life of a waterman.

Gareth skimmed along the quiet river past old homes built on the bank's wooded hillsides. He glanced up at them. Names of each, etched in his memory from childhood, came to mind. Suddenly, he remembered that Nora worried about him when she was not in the boat. He lifted the oars and sliced the water with rhythmic timing, easy but faster. He had told her he would be home in time for supper.

River life teemed around him. Overhead, a soaring hawk screeched for a mate. From the trees, birds sang of spring. Bank grasses waved in the gentle breeze. Rarely did he have time to enjoy, but today, Gareth was in his element. Gliding along, he thought about a promise made to his wife on the day they were married. Only yesterday, Nora had reminded him. "You said, 'Someday, we'll buy Sparse Bounty and live out our lives there.'"

A water snake slithered past the boat in the opposite direction. He drew in scents of spicy autumn olive and sweet honeysuckles, feeling at one with nature, at peace with himself.

Tiring after some distance, he turned on the boat motor, and the time up-river went faster than he had reckoned for his mind filled with everything around him. He thought the house should be coming into sight now. Looking up to his right, there it was—Sparse Bounty. It fronted the river from a gentle knoll below the hillside. A quiet place, like other Wicomico homes, it was some distance from neighbors.

Sparse Bounty sat in full sunshine, causing light to bounce from dormer panes and the storm door. Two chimneys, one on each end, rose above the curb roof. At one time, the now faded hue of the clapboard was moss green with darker trim.

Cutting the motor, Gareth took up the oars and pushed against the bottom to align the boat against the dock. He tied up, and sat studying Sparse Bounty. Dating from the early 1800s, it rested on brick pillars, and from his position, Gareth could see a few of the foundation supports. He thought they looked sturdy enough and would not need much work. He figured he and Nora would have plenty of time to do what had to be done after they retired.

He took in the length and breadth of the house. The roof shingles might need replacing. Four dormers across the front roof appeared to need no repair, as did the four tall shuttered windows and wide front door. An airline pilot and his wife from Washington, D. C., made renovations then vacated the property several years ago. They had added a storm door beneath the cap-covered entrance. Left it in good condition, he thought, noticing added step banisters.

Gareth stepped over the side of the boat and walked up the knoll toward the house. What stories could this old place tell? He thought how, over the years, this particular house pulled at Nora in some strange way that neither of them could explain.

"I feel some connection," she had said, "like I belong there."

Gareth wanted his wife to have this place, and he felt he would be happy here too. Nora worked with him on the boat on days when cleaning and laundry did not have her attention. A robust woman, she was most always pleasant and did not mind hard work. She is my love, he thought, pausing closer in to inspect the area.

At the front steps, century-old boxwood shrubs gave off their distinct odor. Paint flaked from the clapboards in places due to fierce winters. Walking to the back, he stood gazing up at the wood-line. Mature trees dotted the far-back knoll. Apparently former owners planted holly, dogwood and crepe myrtles. Well-groomed front and back lawns welcomed guests from land or water. Gareth guessed Tom hired someone to mow the grass.

When Tom Jenkins, the realtor, handed him the door key, Gareth asked him to say nothing to Nora. "I don't want her to know I'm looking at Sparse Bounty."

Now glancing right, then left, he noticed a car path leading up the slope. It ended at an old, unpainted building more recently used for a garage. From the tree line, another less-used trail led to the river. He imagined many a tobacco cask pushed by Maryland slaves from the tobacco field down the "rolling road" to the plantation pier.

The original dock underwent rebuilds several times in Gareth's lifetime.

Walking down slope, he stopped to look up at the rear of the house. Two dormers highlighted the back roof, and on the lower level, shuttered, average-sized windows fit on either side of the middle entrance. Yep, this is Nora's dream.

Between years of Sparse Bounty standing empty, several industrious young couples revived it at different times. He and Nora made many trips up the Wicomico in the workboat to harvest rockfish and admire the house, but they were never inside.

Lots of history in this old place, Gareth thought, as he returned to the front and unlocked the entrance. Stepping through the heavy door, he walked around the downstairs. Back at the walnut staircase, he stood, rubbing his hand over the smooth newel post. Then, taking the stairs to the first landing, he paused and looked up to the ceiling. "Gosh darn. That panel's been cut," he muttered. An almost indiscernible saw line in the wide walnut panel looked tacky. Have to replace the whole panel. Where will I find a walnut board that width?

Remembering a short ladder seen beneath the house, he went for it.

Back inside, he positioned it on the landing and climbed up, warning himself to take care not to fall because Nora did not know his whereabouts.

Gareth pushed at the top of the panel. Nothing moved. He pushed on the saw line. Then, pushing hard at the top again, the tight fit swung out at the lower cut end, opening to a space the size of a rural mailbox. Unable to see inside, he reached halfway to his elbow and felt something. With a hand around it, he pulled the heavy parcel out.

Stepping down the ladder, he sat on the landing with the bundle across his knees and puzzled over what secret required hiding behind the wall. Gingerly, he unfolded a frayed, yellowed towel to a book of fragile pages and . . . silverware! He counted eight of each piece. Why did no one before me see the cut and have curiosity about the scar on the panel? Without much interest in the tableware, he laid the silverware aside and began reading the journal.

Gareth had read for some time when he noticed the position of the sun. Climbing up the ladder, he pushed the panel piece back in place and returned the ladder outside. Then, back inside, he thought of his good fortune that others had not discovered the treasure. Gathering up the towel-wrapped silver, he did a quick tour through the upstairs rooms. Back downstairs, he walked out and locked the door.

On the river again, Gareth sped along, taking in deep breaths. Excitement was hard to contain in his rush to reveal his discovery to Nora.

He had met no one on his up-river trip and did not expect to see anyone on the way down, but there ahead was old Charley Shatner, puttering up in his workboat. Gareth cut his motor, knowing Charley would have something to say.

"Hey, Gareth!" He waved and turned off his motor. "Did you see them?"

"See who, Charley?"

"Why the people that bought Sparse Bounty."

Gareth's shoulders drooped as the boat rocked in the water.

"They paid three hundred thousand dollars for it. I thought I might see them up there." Charley wiped his face with a rag. "What you doing out here in that outboard?"

"No." Gareth squinted, ignoring Charley's last question. "No, I ain't seen anybody." Not wanting his friend to know where he had been, he said, "I have a ways to go yet, Charley. See you." With disappointment resting in his mind like a dark cloud, he restarted the motor. Glad he had not told Nora of his plans, he glanced at the bundle and reminded himself to turn up the speed.

Back at the crab house pier, he tied-up and driving across the bridge to Cobb Island, he glanced at the back of his house on the sound side. Nora would be starting supper.

He parked the truck, removed the journal and silver bundle, and entered the house.

"Hey!" Nora called from the sink where she pared potatoes. "Have a good day?"

"Yeah, sorta." Gareth slumped on a chair at the kitchen table. "Sort of good and bad."

Nora ran water over the potatoes and put the pot on the burner.

"Hon, when you finish there, come sit down. I have things to tell and show you."

She dried her hands and sat down beside Gareth.

He placed the bundle on the table and told her where he had been. "I have good news," he said, tapping the wrapped silverware, "but first I want to tell you what Charley said."

Nora's face showed gloom on hearing Sparse Bounty again belonged to new owners.

"We should have bought that house before now." Gareth pushed back in his chair, bent forward and propped on his knees.

"No. No shouldas, Gareth. We decided to retire first." Nora placed work-roughened hands over his. "'Them city folks don't stay long anyway. They move down here thinking they like country living and soon decide it ain't exciting enough. We'll have another chance to buy my house." She smiled reassurance and indicating the towel-wrapped packet before her, she asked, "What do you have here?"

Gareth smiled. "That's my girl. Nora, you ain't gonna believe this." Holding out the journal, he said her great aunt wrote it during the Civil War. "You never mentioned an Aunt Nell Spencer."

"I didn't know I had an Aunt Nell. Spencers owned Sparse Bounty way back, but I didn't know they were kin," Nora said. "You suppose that's why I feel close to Sparse Bounty? How is it I didn't know about an Aunt Nell?"

"Hon," Gareth put an arm over her shoulders, "cause . . . well, Nell married a Spencer and moved to Philadelphia before the war. An abolitionist group asked them to return to Maryland and help the Union. Her husband Lance bought Sparse Bounty, built the box to hold her treasures and cut a hole in the walnut panel to hide her journal and her mother's silver. In the journal, she writes that she and her brother, William Lindsey, were born to Mason and Ellen Lindsey. Nora, your great-grandpa was William Lindsey. She wrote that their father Mason built Sparse Bounty, but her brother William, a gambling man, lost it in a poker game."

Nora laughed, looking happy again. "Well that's interesting. My parents told many stories about my Lindsey grandparents, but I know nothing about my great-grandparents. My folks would never have mentioned any gambling kin. And they never mentioned a Nell."

"Probably because she and her husband lived some distance from here." Gareth reminded Nora that her Lindsey kin sympathized with the South during the Civil War.

"You will want to read this journal later, but let me tell you what Nell Spencer recorded about helping runaway slaves who crossed the Potomac and needed to get up North. She passed messages to the Union side about southern sympathizers in southern Maryland. Nell put the messages in a beaver pelt bag and stuck them in a knothole in a dock post." She wrote that a storm tore up the dock after the war, and her husband had it cut into fireplace wood.

"I guess I won't be mentioning about my northern sympathizers." Nora grinned. She picked up a silver fork and admired the scrolled 'L' on the handle. "Someday, Gareth, Sparse Bounty will be in the hands of family again." Her face cast a happy glow.

"Yeah. I believe it will." Gareth leaned back. He felt rewarded by his day up river and with a most understanding woman in his life. Silently, he made a promise to himself and Nora. Tomorrow he intended to visit the realtor. If Sparse Bounty came on the market again, he must be the first to know.

MEED TO A PEAR TREE

$\mathscr{B}$IDDY BREATHED IN AND OUT, bringing the delicate sweetness of summer fruit into her nostrils. If I could make up one true sentence, she thought, it would be about the joy of sitting here neath this tree early in the evening. I would make a sentence about a place I didn't have to toil over.

After finishing a long day of housecleaning at Miz Kate's, she needed a rest. Biddy liked Miz Kate well enough, but mind you, housework five days a week was work.

On summer days, a fresh mellow breeze carried her from the musty task of dusting Miz Kate's antique furniture into a craving reverence. It was then that the neglected, unshapely pear tree beckoned her to sit beneath it.

Most days, Biddy took a pear from the tree and ate it as she hurried home where work still awaited her. Today, she sat on the ground, backed against the tree trunk. She looked up into the straggly branches and above her hung the perfect fruit—the pear of the day.

Struggling to her feet, she stretched as far as she could on her tiptoes and pulled the sunlit yellow fruit from its mother's hold. "Don't you be crying, Momma Tree, cause I be tugging on you." For a moment, she stood rubbing the smooth, leather-like skin. "Smooth as a baby's bottom," she said, sliding back down the tree trunk to the ground. Before biting into it, she wondered how nature made so many shapes. Holding the stem end of the pear, she thought it resembled a banjo. It sho have a big round bottom . . . not a'tall like my Hottentot butt, she thought.

She laughed aloud at her thoughts, allowing them to take her inward. After a day's work, her body felt like a worn wound, tired and aching down her spine. Like the stem of this pear, she thought. Maybe it be tired too, hanging up there in the hot sun . . . growing more softer and more sugary, and waiting for me to come sit under this tree.

Turning the pear, she saw a brown slash on one side. Juice oozed from the injury like sweat from her pores. Maybe this pear be shaped like a tear, so when we tasting the buttery goodness, we be remembering all the sadness in this old world. Well, I ain't gonna think bout no sadness today.

She skimmed off a small area with her teeth and bit into the squishy flesh. Juice dripped and ran along her fingers. The flavor melted over her tongue and flowed velvety into her throat.

Biddy cleared another portion of skin away with her teeth and chomped into the fruit again. Wonder what this pear be feeling? If it not be too tired from turning ripe for me, it be feeling good about making me want to keep on sloshing into one bite after another.

"Um-m." Like Miz Kate be telling me how good I clean.

She chewed around the fibrous inner stem and the opaque shell-like cover protecting the seeds. With her palate sated, Biddy pitched the core. Pushing up from the ground, she wiped the back of her hand across her mouth and swiped it down her plaid, gathered skirt.

Starting homeward, she stopped and looked back. "Now, Miz Pear Tree, don't you go anywhere 'cause I be coming back tomorrow for the tasty sweetness you bear for me."

PROMISES WITHIN REACH

ANNA MAE HACKETT SAT BESIDE the well house, gazing across at Shadowcast Mountain. The hollow between Old Humpback and Shadowcast ran deep and wide. To reveal herself to the other side of her world, Anna Mae hollered across the chasm. "Anna Mae's gonna be a teacher." Sighing, she stared at the sun-sparked boulders, noticing how the morning sun brightened the face of Shadowcast. The boulders are strong, she thought. They are blinking promises back at me. Her face lit up. "Yep," she said aloud, "this is the day for promises made to myself."

Anna Mae hollered across the valley again. "This is the day! Yep, this is the day."

She rose from the wooden bucket where she had sat contemplating her chances, straightened her back and gingham dress, and trooped to the cabin door.

In the bedroom shared with two younger sisters, she threw the sum of her wardrobe—a few more gingham dresses and other necessities—into a cloth bag.

Her mother knew of her plans to leave, but not when. Now packed and ready, Anna Mae stepped up beside her in the kitchen. "I'm going, Mama. This is the time."

"Yes, child. Go fore yore daddy gits home." They embraced, and Anna Mae strode out the door, threw the bag over her shoulder and headed down the mountain path.

"Gonna be a teacher. Gonna be, gonna be." Walking apace of her tune, she kept up the cadence on the valley road toward the Ozark town of Obeah. The community college campus was her goal. Suddenly it occurred to her that she did not have a dime on her person. Okay, what you gonna do now? "I'll know when I get there," she said, with a bit less confidence than she felt.

She reached the college campus as darkness fell, tired and with no money to bargain for lodging. She came upon one building set back from the long-running sidewalk. In the building's shadowy alcove, Anna Mae dropped her bag, curled into the niche and rested her head on the bundle. She dozed until a harsh voice awakened her.

"Hey, Boze! There's a . . ." A flashlight beam blinded her. "There's a gal sleeping over here." Another security guard walked up and stood looking down at Anna Mae as she struggled to get up.

"What you doing here, girl? It don't make no difference." The guards laughed. "We gonna have to haul you over to the station. Get your stuff and let's go."

"I'm here to start school—"

"No need telling us now. Wait till we get to the station so we can write it in our report."

Anna Mae's heart drummed a rapid beat. She wanted to cry, but she would not.

At the station, one of the guards wrote down her story. Then he said she could rest in one of the chairs until morning.

When the police shift changed at seven o'clock, she asked one of the fresh guards how to find the campus cafeteria. He directed her and she headed out.

In the cafeteria, she walked up to the first worker she saw. "How do I get a job here?"

The girl rolled her eyes. "Go back there and see Miss Mabel. She does all the hiring."

Anna Mae stood in the doorway, drawing conclusions about Miss Mabel, who stood at a table chopping cabbage with a cleaver. Oh heck. This ain't gonna be easy, she thought, walking over to the woman. "Miss Mabel?"

Appearing middle-aged, the orange-haired woman wearing a hairnet spun around to reveal a grimacing ruddy face. "Yeah, what you want?"

"Uh . . . uh, Miss Mabel, I'm going to enroll in Home Ec classes and I need a job—"

"You ever been hired as a cook? Worked in a cafe . . . any experience a 'tall?"

"No ma'am, just cooking at home for my family."

"Then what makes you think you can work here?"

Anna Mae felt desperate. She gazed at the hard woman and wondered how to bring her around. "Ma'am, I am going to start school here. Someday, I'm going to teach Home Economics. I'm gonna do it even if I don't have a dime to my name. Do you know where I *might* get a job?"

Miss Mabel smiled and told her to get the apron and hairnet hanging on a wall hook. "Put them on and come help me make coleslaw."

At the end of day, worn from the long walk, no sleep and eight hours of work, Anna Mae trudged into the registrar's office. A nameplate on the desk read, Everett Douglass. "I'm here to enroll, Mr. Douglass." Anna Mae let her cloth bag slip to the floor at her feet.

The elderly man looked at her as though he disapproved of her gingham dress and cloth bag. "The office is closing. Come back tomorrow." Adjusting his tie, he returned to his writing.

"I have no place to come back from. No place to even go." Anna Mae muttered more to herself than to him. She pushed long black curls behind her ears, hooked her arm through her bag, and turned to leave.

"Wait a minute. What did you say?" The man laid the pen aside.

Anna Mae repeated that she had no place to go, but she intended to go to school.

He gazed at her face that must have shown her sadness. "Sit down." He invited her to tell about herself. When she paused after telling of growing up on Shadowcast Mountain, dreaming of being an Home Economics teacher and walking to Obeah, he stood and walked to a coat rack. "Come with me. Mrs. Douglass will be happy to have a pretty young girl in the house."

Anna Mae, a bit taken aback by his thinness and height, followed without question.

They walked across the campus and several streets to arrive at the Douglass home.

Mr. Douglass introduced Anna Mae to his wife. They took seats in the living room and he repeated much of what the young girl had told him.

Anna Mae read kindness in the white-haired woman's pretty face. Some malady had left her stooped.

Mrs. Douglass struggled up from the chair, hooked her cane over one arm, and told Anna Mae to bring her bag and follow her to a bedroom. There, as best she could, Mrs. Douglass enfolded her in a welcoming embrace.

After a warm bath and dinner, Anna Mae told the elderly couple she was determined to go to school and become a teacher. "I want to go back to my mountain and teach girls how to be better wives and mothers."

They listened to her plans, and Mrs. Douglass said, "Dear, I would like to see you broaden your view." She said that teaching young mountain girls to be better wives and mothers was a commendable aspiration. "Anna Mae, you have courageously reached out to the world. Why not major in Home Ec and minor in English or Sociology? Prepare yourself to teach your students to see the world beyond Shadowcast Mountain. I have an idea. Why don't you stay with us?"

She turned to her husband, and he agreed. Mr. Douglass said if Anna Mae was up to it after work at the cafeteria, she could help his wife. "She has rheumatoid arthritis and is limited in what she can do. Your pay will be lodging and food. How does that sound?"

"Why I'm used to hard work. I can't believe my luck, but there is one other thing. I have no money for tuition and books. Is there any way I can pay after I've made enough money?"

"Yes, we will work that out," Mr. Douglass said. "Do you think you can pass the SATs, the math and English tests? They aren't easy, and you must make an average score to be admitted."

"I'm willing to try. If I don't pass the first time, can I try again?"

"Well, yes you may."

"You know what?" Anna Mae felt her smile reaching out to a bright future. "I knew there were promises at the bottom of Shadowcast Mountain."

All had a good laugh, and Mrs. Douglass said, "Come, Anna Mae. I know you are tired, dear, and you have a full day ahead of you."

OLD NICK'S LEGACY

LD NICK LEFT US LAST Friday.

Old and quite worn out, he had another problem he just could not handle.

Nick lived a blissful life for many years, lazing or grazing in green pastures. His best days were those when Farmer Brown turned him in with the beauties. He reveled and pleasured on those days. Yes, he reigned supreme in his pasture kingdom filled with pretty cows.

Old Nick left a legacy of the many offspring he sired. Some were spitting images of him. Others picked up the spots of a Holstein or the tan of a Jersey. Oh yeah, Old Nick lived a great life until the day old Farmer Brown decided he must be neutered. He could not cope with his new status among the cows and simply gave up the ghost.

Farmer Brown hauled his lifeless carcass off to a ravine and dumped it. The farmer just left him there for the vultures to pick.

It was a heck of a way for the proud bull of the herd to go.

AUNT ALICE'S TREAT

*G*REAT-AUNT ALICE INVITED ME INTO a cozy kitchen warmed by a wood-burning range. The relative I was seeing for the first time directed me to a chair.

A nutty aroma tempted me and attracted my eyes to a baking sheet atop the stove. It held hot roasted peanuts, not long from the oven. I craved those nuts and remembered standing before the candy jar in the drugstore. Mr. Hurst had pushed peppermints across the counter to me.

Aunt Alice smiled sweet as sugar and pointed to the pan. "Have some peanuts." I felt safe with the motherly woman whose dark hair pinned in a bun at her nape.

I sat for a moment, questioning my manners. Should I accept the tempting offer or decline with "No, thank you?" Unable to resist my craving, I slipped off the chair and sidled over to the pan. Scooping up hourglass shapes in both hands and fearful of dropping even one of them, I returned with care to my chair at the table. Cracking a papery shell between my teeth, I pulled the fibrous wrapping apart at the seam. Staring down, I saw two stone-like red gems cradled in half of their protective pod. I moved the cradle to my open mouth and rolled the peanuts into it.

Aunt Alice gave me quick glances and approving smiles, and with each crunchy bite, I felt greatly comforted in the company of my great-aunt.

FLOATING MYSTERY

A LIGHT OILY FRAGRANCE DRIFTED FROM some unknown source. Citron wisely used? Perhaps. So light the scent, its flavor remained indistinguishable.

Sightless, I sat sniffing, trying to determine the exactness of such pleasure. I knew something desirable had just passed before me. A freshly bathed and lotioned lady? Yes, she is a refined woman, wearing her essence in such a way that a trail of mystery floats behind her.

Six months on the sands of Iraq, I wished for such delight. Conjuring up a beauty, so close I could feel her lightly oiled skin, warmness flooded my body. Sitting in the crowded waiting room of the international airport terminal, I told myself it was a passing thing.

Taping my cane, I grew more impatient with each moment.

FEMMES ON THE CUSP

$\mathcal{M}$ARTHA HEAVED HERSELF OUT OF the city cab onto the sidewalk. She tucked fare into the cabby's hand and glanced at the canopy over the entrance to the posh Connecticut Avenue restaurant. "Co Co's," she muttered. Assured she had landed at the right place, Martha straightened her dress. Trusting it defied her weight, she walked through the door held open by a nattily dressed man. She smiled, said "Thank you," and checked her watch. "Blast! Twenty minutes late."

Martha considered promptness one of her sterling qualities.

Waiting for the hostess, she thought about how little time she and her two friends had during their monthly luncheons. She recalled Jill and Adriana's surprise last month when she offered no support for the Women's Liberation Movement.

She thought that topic still unfinished when the hostess appeared, interrupting her recollection. "The Threesome Party," Martha said, just as a waving yellow napkin caught her attention. "Ah, there." She tapped the woman on the shoulder and indicated the table where Adriana and Jill sat. Good, she thought, on seeing her friends seated away from the other diners. We will not worry about being overheard.

The three had met like this since the sixties. They were neighbors then, living in the same southern Maryland suburb and taking turns hosting lunch in their homes. After Martha's adult children left for college, she and Howard moved into a Virginia townhouse. Around that time, her friend Jill Mercer landed a job with Metro Transit Authority's publicity department. Jill and her husband Scott bought a renovated row house in Washington, D. C.

Separated by distance, they now met monthly at a selected restaurant.

Having taken leave of Maryland in 1971, Martha tried to convince the Beckhams to make a change in location. She told Howard her words were ignored. "Adriana and Niles will never move from that rural environment. Niles is always doing things to the house. He amazes me . . . commuting downtown everyday to his government job." She went on to tell her husband how Jill needled Adriana about two of her four sons still living at home. "Jill says those boys are in their mid-twenties—too old for the nest, but Howard, Adriana will never kick her kids out. No matter that she yearns for city lights, the theater, museum lectures and fine eateries."

Now, following the hostess, Martha remembered next month was her turn to arrange lunch.

Approaching her friends, she looked around in an approving manner. "Adriana, you found a perfect place." Aware of her shrill voice, she added above a whisper, "It's lovely here." Then as she considered propriety another of her sterling qualities, she apologized for being late. Hanging her handbag on the chair arm, she rushed on. "Lots of traffic at the Tidal Basin. Tourists you know, cherry blossom season." She caught a breath between fractured sentences, and like a hen settling on a nest, arranged herself on the paisley-covered padding of the chair.

Over the years, the three friends had shared their children's growing pains, and on some occasions, their own marriage crises. Held together by those bonds, only last month over coq au vin and white wine at Shamon's, they had discussed the full-blown feminist movement.

After listening to Jill and Adriana's agreements with Gloria Steinem and Bella Abzug, Martha had said, "At my age, I'm comfortable with the way things are. We are just three middle-aged women caught on the edge of this feminine revolution."

Now, settled at the table, she adjusted her weight on the chair and reopened the subject. "Women's Lib is really revving up. It's all happening too fast for our generation." She unfolded her napkin and laid it across her lap. "I can't see myself burning my bra—"

"You rant against marching, chanting and talk about burning bras," Jill said, wrinkling her brow. "Come on, Martha. Our age puts us on the cusp of a generational change. We are caught between old servile ways and taking up our own individuality. Why shouldn't we be the persons we are?" She threw out a challenge to the other two. "Let's make a life-altering decision! Today, right now." She paused, glancing from one to the other of her friends. "Actually, I have."

She glared at Adriana, pointing to her ring finger. "Looks like you have too, Adriana. Thought I wouldn't notice, didn't you?" Jill looked at Martha, "See this, her hand?"

Martha watched Adriana fuss with her napkin and drop her hand to her lap.

Adriana faced Jill's stare. "Yes. Well, it has come to this. I have a plan that will end—"

"Oh-h Adriana, not divorce?" Martha frowned. "You just can't give up everything!"

"Dear, I don't know how else—"

"Are you telling us . . ." Remembering where she was, Martha lowered her voice. "Are you ready to give up thirty years of marriage?" She searched her friend's face, knowing its dark complexion would not show a blush. Without waiting for an explanation, she pled in a mere whisper. "You're smart, dear. I say, live with what you have. It's the safe way." In her normal voice, she said, "I've studied divorce up one side and down the other. Ask yourself, Adriana, 'Will an annuity check arrive in the mail if my ex dies or remarries?'"

She looked at her friend, waiting for an answer. When there was not one coming, she declared, "It will all go to a second wife. Believe me, a man will find another woman!" Martha felt her blood pressure rising and fanned her face with the napkin.

Adriana's face screwed into confusion.

Jill fingered the lapel of her royal purple jacket. "We're expected to stay home, take care of husbands and kids. Women are in a quandary, and I deal with it better than you two."

Martha thought Jill struggled for a more gentle remonstrance, but as usual, her take-charge manner prevailed. "Martha, what makes you think you know what's best for Adriana?"

"Well, I think we're stupid to give up the security we've earned in thirty-year marriages. We are entitled to it and I'm not altering my lifestyle. Adriana has to make Niles and the boys understand that her identity lacks fulfillment in her roles of wife and motherhood." Martha bent toward her friend. "Tell them you need time outside the home, Adriana. I've watched your 'supermom' act." Martha made quote marks in the air, picked up a carrot stick and gave it a vigorous chew while smearing a thick piece of bread with sweet butter.

Jill turned a goblet of white wine between ring-adorned hands. Told she had lovely hands, she had said they were her best feature boxed in an otherwise large bone structure. Blonde hair, blue eyes and fair skin were dead giveaways of Jill's Nordic ancestry. Resting the glass, she said, "Your anger does show, Adriana. Where does it get you? Your kids are used to it and ignore you. And dear old undiscerning Niles thinks it is menopause."

"I know, Jill. I mumble angry thoughts to myself. Oh, damn! Martha, I do let them know." Adriana slipped into the frustrated mood Martha knew all too well. "I've told them time and time again." Her distorted face detracted from the sophisticated image she created in a fuchsia coatdress and narrow-brimmed, black hat resting above a neat chignon. She continued. "I have no grounds for divorce. That's why I've decided to give Niles a reason to divorce me."

An uncomfortable silence followed her declaration of intent, and straightening her shoulders, Adriana sighed. "You're right. Anger is a poor way to deal with boredom, but seeing life parade before my eyes . . . all the disappointments—"

"Come now, Adriana," Martha cajoled. "Look at you, a model's flawless skin. You always look like you stepped onto a Garfinckel runway. Women envy you and men wilt." She rushed on. "Poor old Niles, he must be uneasy all the time. Put that ring back on your finger," she chided in a somewhat playful manner.

Adriana gazed at her. "Did it ever occur to you, Martha, that good looks can be a problem? Appreciation for having some depth would be nice." She said she took an advertising job to see if she could still do something more than clean and be a mother. "I was so pleased." She wiped a welling tear and blew into a tissue. "Well, you know what happened. Niles began drinking, and I was forced to give up the job." She said Niles claimed he was ready to retire, and with her working, he would be home alone every day.

Jill placed her hand over Adriana's. "Let Niles be responsible for his drinking. He decided to drink, but you are to blame for giving up your job. He didn't force you—"

"I faced a decision! Give up the job or leave him. I couldn't leave. Didn't make enough money to support myself, and I wanted to stay married for the boys' sake."

"I'm not defending Niles, Adriana. He seems to need you more than you need him."

Adriana turned to Jill and said she was right as usual. "That's why I'm about to . . . don't you see? I intend to take charge of my life." She blew into the tissue again. "Isn't that what Women's Lib is all about? Isn't that what you did when you began an affair with Ned what's-his-name? Scott still thinks he has a faithful wife. I am just taking charge, as you did. Catch a man, *then* . . ."

Watching Adriana regain her demeanor and push away her half-eaten salad, Martha emitted an exasperated sigh. She straightened the napkin tucked into the front of her navy blue dress and craved the unfinished salad. Pushing graying red hair behind her ear, she sighed and followed Adriana's interest in four men in coats and ties several tables away. She watched the play between Adriana and one of them. They stared at each other across the distance.

Turning to her friends, Adriana whispered, "I knew it would pay to come here where classy men dine. Don't look now, but handsome—the one in the gray jacket—is facing this way."

Waiting a plausible moment, Martha noted the spread of enthusiasm all over Adriana's face and turned for a discreet look at the man.

Jill looked over her shoulder. "Dark blue shirt shows taste."

"Suppose he's married?" Adriana's face showed surprise, as though she had just thought of such a possibility.

"Bet on it." Martha eyed Adriana's uneaten salad. Silently chastising herself for craving it, she returned to her friend's question. "Any good man left has a female hanging onto him."

Jill nodded. "He's married. Has a ring on his finger." She dismissed Adriana's attraction to defend her own illicit affair. "Listen, I played around with Ned but it wasn't a purposeful decision to do so. It just happened." She turned the rings on her fingers and told how she took him down from the shelf, played a few hours and put him away until the next time. "It was fun to flirt over lunch, to throw responsibility to the wind. How long has it been since you two had fun?"

Martha chewed on a carrot stick and did not try to answer.

Adriana shook her head as though she could not remember when. Then, "Maybe it was the last time we had lunch." She laughed, as if she had made a joke.

"Yeah, I thought so," Jill said. "Anyway, Ned is history. I'm not advising you to try what I did, but don't knock it." She turned her rings, declaring that men fooled around and at some point, women deserved to be as free as they were. "Be more than Mrs. Someone."

Martha thought Jill appeared pleased with her metaphor for a wife.

Jill continued. "Listen, I've given thought to what I want life to be for Scott and me."

Just then, the waiter appeared for the condiment dish and salad plates. Before he could take them away, Martha grabbed the last carrot stick.

He returned with entrees.

"Scallops Delmonico with a glass of Chablis, um-m," Martha grunted and sipped wine.

Without waiting to hear Jill's thoughts, she began relating her own problems. "I never told you this, but Howard wants a tumble in bed every night. Yeah, at his age!" She was happy to turn him over to his mistress, but to get involved with another man, that was not for her. "I'm telling you, you two are going to be losers." She popped a scallop in her mouth. Swallowing, she looked at Jill. "You're lucky Scott hasn't learned about Ned. It's just a matter of time. He will throw you out with nothing. No home, car, no equity in his estate."

Martha told how she kept up with changes in divorce laws, especially those that set precedents in the division of property. She reminded them they were not in California where wives received half of the common property. Raising her eyebrows, she said, "Get acquainted with the state law before you go off on wild tangents. As I told you before, I married for security. What is love? I have lived thirty-four years without it, but I respect Howard as the father of our kids. He has provided for us quite nicely. I'll stick by him."

Martha turned to Adriana and thought she appeared more interested in the man across the way than in what she had said. Nevertheless, she continued between chews. "Call it life-altering or whatever, I'm opening a nice little bank account in my name in case Howard leaves me high and dry. Will you two co-sign it? If something happens to me, give the money to my kids."

"Come off it, Martha! I know why you stay with Howard." Jill's patience sounded exhausted. "Look, my friend, I'm going to tell you what your problem is." Glancing around, she softened her voice. "Not to be unkind . . . If you stop eating for *one moment*, perhaps this will sink in. It's sad but true, Martha. You eat too much."

Martha stopped chewing, rested her fork on the plate, and saw Adriana gape at Jill.

"I've tried to say this before," Jill said, "beneath that excess poundage is a beautiful person who lacks self-confidence. I think you eat because you are unhappy with yourself. Why don't you find some up-to-date training? Get a job?" Jill steamed on as if she stopped now she would never say it. "You stay with Howard because you think you don't have a ghost of a chance with another man. Guess what! You two just tolerate each other. Do you want life—?"

"Oh, Jil-l, did you have to say those things?" Martha eyes teared. Clapping a hand on each side of her face, she picked up the napkin and dabbed her eyes. Gaining control, she caught a distraught look on Adriana's face as she and Jill consoled with gentle pats on her arms.

Jill appeared to ache for her, even as she pressed on. "It's true, Martha. Accept the truth. Your health concerns us. I care about you and want you to face up to your own future." She removed her hand from Martha's arm.

Martha made a gruntled sound. "You're a psychiatrist now?" she said, giving Jill an accusatory look.

Apparently, the question startled Jill, but she quickly regained dominance. "No, Martha, but let me tell you something surprising." The other two perked up, and she rushed on. "I was ashamed to tell anyone. Not even you two, that Scott's been unfaithful all of our married life."

"Oh, Jil-l, I didn't guess." Martha gave over the sympathy she had always felt for Scott.

Adriana reached a hand to Jill, but withdrew, perhaps knowing her friend did not respond to shows of emotion.

"For years I loved that man," Jill continued, "hardly able to bear what I knew. Ashamed. Well, now you know and here's the deal. I am responsible for my own happiness. Ned and I are finished." She raised a warning hand before they could say anything. "Wait! Get this." Voice barely audible, she said, "I made a decision and I'm happy!"

Both friends looked astounded and confused, and Jill appeared to think her state of happiness might be hard to believe. "I've released Scott, stopped possessing him. Claiming him as 'mine.'" She made illustrated quotes in the air. "Funny, I can't remember ever being so unburdened. What do you think?"

Bewildered, Martha said, "She's been to a shrink." She glinted at Adriana. For a moment, neither she nor Adriana seemed to know what to say. Then, "I didn't even guess, Jill," Martha said, as the waiter presented the dessert menu. "Uh, let's have chocolate mousse—"

"No," the other two said in unison, and Jill held up two fingers. "Two coffees."

"I'll have the mousse," Martha told him, and feeling defiant, she smiled at her friends.

"Have your mousse, girl. If you will not listen about yourself, then hear this. Scott and I agreed to stay married just for the family's sake." She looked to them as if seeking a reaction. "Guess what. I can't recall when we've been more content. He is home every night. It's like we've been released from prison." Jill rushed on. "Scott said something really profound. He said, 'I don't feel like a possession, so I'm free to love you.' Think about that, Adriana. Talk to Niles."

Adriana sipped coffee, and Martha ate mousse. They observed Jill check her watch, stand, and dig in her handbag for money. "I can't finish my coffee. Must run, girls, management-level meeting in thirty minutes. This should cover me." Placing bills on the table, she waved.

For a few moments, the other two sat without speaking. Adriana stole another glance at "Handsome." He stared back with a bold smile, and Martha broke the spell. "Do you think she's really happy? Jill, I mean. You know, I thought I had you and Jill all figured out. She fooled around, and you, Adriana, were the faithful homemaker. Somehow, it wouldn't surprise me if Jill and Scott come out of this with a sound marriage after all."

"Uh huh." Adriana stirred and sipped with a look that showed her mind was elsewhere.

"Are you going to wear your ring?"

"I'll put it on before I get home, Martha, but I intend to make some changes. This is a good restaurant, isn't it? Shall we come here again next month?" Her intention seemed set.

Touching her friend's arm, Martha interrupted Adriana's bemused gaze and tried to assess the depth of her desire to stray. Sighing, she pushed away the half-eaten mousse.

Adriana watched the four men rise from their table. Handsome veered toward them, and she dropped her napkin to the floor. He bent, picked it up and smiled down at her. "I believe you dropped this, gorgeous."

Martha, observing the flash of electricity between them, sighed again. For a moment, she felt a twinge of envy, and then her need for security erased it. If like Jill, Adriana would be satisfied with a fleeting flirtation, she could accept that as long as her friend remained with Niles and his support.

RHINESTONES ARE
A GAL'S BEST FRIEND

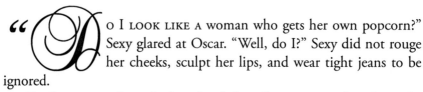

"**D**O I LOOK LIKE A woman who gets her own popcorn?" Sexy glared at Oscar. "Well, do I?" Sexy did not rouge her cheeks, sculpt her lips, and wear tight jeans to be ignored.

For forty years, Oscar had made a habit of not ignoring her. Since the day the big galoot asked her for a first date, he had called Maxine "Sexy." A marine then, straight out of boot camp, he enjoyed leave in Texas before shipping out to a new assignment.

That was then, and now they stood in the lobby of the movie theater beside the Town Mall. Sexy glanced around the lobby for onlookers—her audience. Only two high school kids, heads together, giggled behind the concession counter. Totally into themselves, she thought.

She thought her pale face might show her disappointment, a stark contrast framed in black hair. But being her normal in-charge self, she stepped over empty popcorn bags and candy wrappers scattered about the floor, and waited beside the popcorn vending machine. Pounding on the counter, she turned and called, "Oscar!"

Oscar walked over to Sexy. His rhinestone-trimmed leather jacket glittered under the lights. "Why, honey bunch, do I look like the kind of guy that would let my rhinestone gal buy her own popcorn?" Grinning at the gaping kid behind the counter, he patted Sexy on the derriere and pulled his wallet from a back pocket of his jeans.

Sexy, holding a bucket of popcorn in the circle of her arm and a large Coke in her hand, walked a few steps from the counter. She stopped, waiting for Oscar, and smiled at five or six people who had just entered the lobby.

Oscar joined her, and she strutted toward the auditorium when her three-inch heel snagged on a threadbare spot in the carpet. Sexy did a belly flop onto the floor. Clutching the half-emptied pail, her face buried in spilled popcorn and Coke splashed into her beehive hairdo.

"Oh my, is she hurt?" People gathered around, bending over her.

Oscar fell to his knees. "Honey bunch, are you all right? Let me help you. I hope you ain't broke no part of that gorgeous body."

"Oh, Oscar, shut your mouth and help me turn over."

He rolled her onto her back and pulled her into a sitting position.

She moaned. Strands of sticky hair escaped her beehive and clung to her face. Hearing giggles from the teenagers behind the counter, her eyes filled with tears. Still clutching the pail in one hand and Coke in the other, she said, "Oscar, will you please remove the plug of popcorn from my nose?"

He managed to relieve her of the popcorn plug, and with him and another fellow lifting, Sexy stood on one high heel shoe and one bare foot. Feeling a bedraggled mess, she swished her Coke-held hand at the concerned people around her. "I'm fine. Go on, enjoy the movie." She watched them hesitate then wander toward the darkened entrance. Scanning the floor, she located her shoe. "There it is, Oscar. Can you put it on my foot?"

He stooped to pick up the shoe and found it still caught by the carpet thread. Down on his knees, he untangled the heel, slipped the shoe on Sexy's foot, and clambered up from the floor.

Turning to Oscar, she shoved the popcorn box and plastic drink container at him. 'I'm going to the ladies' room. Get more popcorn and Coke."

Sexy entered the restroom and stood before the mirror. Reflecting back at her was an unbelievable image. She cried. Then, grabbing a handful of paper towels, she wet them, wiped her face and rubbed the sticky out of her hair. Unpinning the beehive, Sexy fluffed her hair and inspected herself in the mirror. She felt in her shoulder bag for blush and lipstick. With fresh rouged cheeks and lips reddened, she looked approvingly at the familiar reflection.

Stepping through the door into the lobby, she thought, I will show them. Lifting her head, she smiled and strolled past the line at the concession counter. Several smiled back at her.

Oscar stood waiting with his arm curled around a popcorn box and a Coke in his hand. With his free hand, he patted Sexy on her derriere. She took Oscar's arm, and turning back to her new audience, gave them a sense of her pride.

FANTASY TAKES FLIGHT

NN SPLASHED A TRAIL OF orange juice, set the glass down before Bob, and back at the kitchen counter, she zapped bacon in the microwave and flipped eggs at the stove. Scooping eggs on his plate, her eyes welled and she sniffled. All night thoughts ran through her head, denying sleep. Anger at her husband pushed guilt for those thoughts far down in her inner soul.

She turned to see Bob take a limp paper napkin and mop the table of spilled juice. Throwing more napkins on the floor, he swept the toe of a polished shoe back and forth between breakfast table and refrigerator.

He looked up at Ann. "Bring your eggs and your coffee, hon. Sit here beside me. I don't want you to worry about me—"

"Don't worry! Will you explain to me how I can keep from worrying?"

Bob gazed at her. His face told her he did not have an answer.

Last evening, weeks after Bob learned of it himself, he blurted out his next assignment. He would have duty on an aircraft carrier in the Persian Gulf.

Times for surprise by such news were long since past. Ann had said nothing, but rattling inside her head was a remark she had heard a thousand times. "Flying is no more dangerous than riding in an automobile." She knew the odds as well as she knew that a loyal military wife would always wear a fixed mask of false bravery.

"Amy and Susan, did they leave for school?"

Their teenage girls were accustomed to their father's comings and goings, and accepted them without questions. Ann nodded and thought he is easing into the same old placating routine. Does he think I'm a limp rag?

Acknowledging her nod, Bob said, "Good." There was a pause, then, "We . . . Ann, it's a whole month before I leave—"

"Listen, Bob! It has been sixteen years and I've had it! It is always the same old tune. 'It won't be long, babe. Don't worry, sweetheart. Nothing's going to happen to me.' It's all about you, Bob. You thrive on danger. You cannot imagine the feeling of being left behind with my life going nowhere. Well, let me tell you—"

"Darling . . ." Looking as if her tears were melting him into putty, he stood and pulled her up into his arms. Raising his napkin, he said, "Here, let me wipe those beautiful brown eyes."

"No, Bob!" She pulled back. "Not this time. Love needs more than 'babes' and 'darlings,' and more than compliments a-and being left behind. Love needs nourishment, a-and wonderful m-memories. T-that's what I need to keep me strong when we're apart." She hid her face in the sleeves of her soft white robe. "I . . . oh-h, I have n-nothing but years of sad departures."

"What about when I come home, Ann? Honey, we will make all those memories together. I promise." Bob pulled her back into his arms, tightening his embrace. "Here now. Sh. Sh-h." He held her for a long moment, then, "I can't eat breakfast. I'm late, Ann. Are you all right?" His grip eased and holding her at arm's length, he waited for a response.

Wiping a sleeve across her eyes, she nodded "yes."

He pulled her close for a quick kiss. "That's my girl. I'll see you tonight." Picking up his flight jacket and cap, at the door he turned, tall, dark-haired and sun-bronzed. "Bye. I love you."

Ann wiped her face with her robe sleeve and lifted her hand in a weak wave. He is so darn predictable. Heaven help him if he is late! Her tears gave way to sarcasm and anger again.

Pitching dirty utensils and their untouched breakfasts in the sink, she whisked around the kitchen, muttering into the silent house. She thought that ended just as it always did. He soothed my ruffled feathers and wriggled his way out of talking about us. All night she had listened to him sleep like a baby. Why should he care that I tossed and turned? I'll show him!

Having washed down the empty sink, she sat in the breakfast nook sipping from a fresh mug of coffee and gazing through the bay window into nothingness as thoughts zipped across her mind. Life is passing me by. Where do I fit? Cooking and cleaning . . . why did I marry him? We are total opposites. Ann wondered how Bob had escaped the tumult of the sixties. I was wild! Wonderful and free . . . He is still free. Just leaves us and goes off to the Persian Gulf. Maybe I don't love him anymore. Do I love him?

A clear answer did not hang in black and white before her eyes. Hand shaking, she drained the coffee cup and dredged up the scenes she had wrestled with throughout the night, trying to rationalize them.

Bob is reserved, no repartee. I knew that when I married him. He is a great family man, stable in a crisis. I need his gentleness to diffuse the girls' upsets. But I need excitement too. To go places . . . be with people. I need to be with him more. Ann pushed hair from her face and brought scenes of their June wedding day into focus. He was dashing in his Marine dress uniform. He still is. It was love at first sight when Timmy introduced him at the academy ball. A momentary smile faded. What would my brother say now, if he knew what I am feeling and thinking?

She had chosen the spiffy guy in uniform. But, she reminded herself, he works by the clock, lives by the rules, enjoys the breakfast service when I don't spill the juice and obligingly pecks me on the cheek before melting into his world.

Ann's head felt ready to explode with nagging whisperings and puzzlements over the contradictions in her life. Her body felt bound up, and she kept coming back to her understanding that Bob did not know her feeling of loneliness.

Such back-and-forth arguing with herself had kept Ann sane at such times, but now, a cold shiver ran through her.

The flagstone path Bob lovingly laid between his flowerbeds suddenly caught her attention. Yep, life should be like that path, wandering among flowers. A bit of uncertainty . . . lots of cultivated beauty, plus a touch of wild color.

A twinge of guilty anticipation raised goose bumps on her arms.

She glanced at the kitchen clock, twenty past eight o'clock. Remembering her sleepless night, she knew circles under her eyes would need plenty of repairs for her twelve noon luncheon date. Suddenly there were wings to her every movement. Cereal boxes from the girls' breakfast landed on a cabinet shelf, but the orange stain on her robe resisted her efforts to rub it out.

Reaching deep into the towel drawer where she stashed her mother's letter, she pulled it out and read it once more. "By the way," her mother wrote, "I saw Mark coming from his office Friday morning. He's flying out to Washington, D. C. next Thursday. Something to do with a case he is defending. He asked for your phone number. Hope it was all right to give it to him."

Her letter rambled on, but Ann was conscious of only the name. Mark Talbott.

Thoughts of Mark and a long ago summer had soothed her raw feelings and placated a marital spat many times. Thinking of him could blur the edge of any upset.

It was June in Georgia. Her term at Weyforth Junior College ended, and Mark came home for the summer from Texas U. He asked her to shoot skeets with him at the Millford range.

Wild flowers lined Sweetbriar Road that day, and trees frilled out in summer green leaves.

Mark may have been an expert rifleman, but what a time he had showing me how to hold and aim that gun. She remembered him telling her to fire just ahead of the clay pigeon and allow for movement.

Mark stood close with his arms around her shoulders. Astounded, her heart had beat like a frantic bird, and she had been unable to concentrate on the clay pigeon.

A flop at skeet, she did not think he would ask her for another date, but later, they walked hand in hand, and picnicked at Old Millstone Lake. Summer grass sparkled with morning dew when they showed up with fishing poles and worms. And laughing . . . we had such fun.

Ann laughed aloud, as if hearing for the first time Mark's imitation of a tree frog.

Mark was not handsome or tall. Sort of pudgy, and freckled with reddish hair. Devilish eyes and crazy ideas. Always surprising me with tales of college pranks, she recalled.

They had dined at the Southern Bell. Gosh, it was small, inexpensive, and nondescript. We didn't need romantic places. Mark wore romance like some men wear machismo.

"Ann, you're a knockout tonight." "Annie Bell! Girl, you make me want to forget everything and just make love to my blond beauty for the rest of my life."

Their last evening, before both returned to school, began reeling out now like an old movie. Then suddenly, Ann was aware of the time. Snapping the dishwasher door shut, she raced upstairs. Mark must have moved up in the world. Sebastian's on Connecticut Avenue was very different from the Southern Bell.

She trembled, remembering their recent phone conversation. "Hello, Ann. Mark Talbott."

"Mark! It's nice to hear from you." She had tried to contain the thrill in her voice. "How's your family?"

"You mean Alicia? She's fine. No children, you know."

"Of . . . of course, I knew."

"Are you still as pretty as I remember? Do you still wear your hair long?"

"It's been a long time, Mark. I am so—"

"Ah, love, you couldn't be anything but beautiful. Come have lunch with me." He chortled, seeming to catch her embarrassment.

"It would be wonderful to see you again, Mark." Ann had felt uncomfortable with the way the conversation went, but at the same time, it had been exhilarating. "Why don't you come out to visit us? It's only thirty miles into Maryland. We'd love to have you." She held her breath for his answer, not really wanting to share Mark with her family.

"I can't possibly, Annie Bell. I'm tied up here and have to leave tomorrow night. Took the liberty of making a reservation at Sebastian's. You know where that is?"

It was just like Mark, charging headlong, full of surprises. "Yes, I know."

He did not have to plead. In a spate of excitement, she had placed down the receiver, not knowing whether to feel happy or guilty. She had walked into the bathroom. A long, close scrutiny of her face in the mirror followed their conversation. She had fretted over discernible crows' feet around her eyes and plucked gray hairs that surely would return twice over.

Now, from the master bedroom closet, Ann pulled a smartly tailored, wool-blend jacket dress, bright blue over black to compliment her coloring and show off her figure. Taking care not to smudge, she covered the dark circles under her eyes, applied blush to her cheeks, and powdered lightly over her nose. She glossed her lips with a hint of color, and swished a brush through her hair, then stood back to study the total effect in the full-length mirror.

Turning slowly, Ann thought smugly that Mark would say she had not changed a bit.

It was eleven o'clock when she grabbed a stole and left Olde Mill, the quaint little village nestled on a Potomac inlet. Thawing February snow patched shaded hillsides and low wooded areas. Ann loved Maryland's rolling hills, hardwood forests and raging brooks sweeping toward the rivers that would empty into the bay.

Driving the speed limit, she hummed to the radio, grateful for the music her girls called "olden days" tunes. Their heavy metal left her longing for Elvis' rock-and-roll. Speeding along, the music was soon lost to thoughts of Mark and their last goodbye.

"You'll write, won't you, Ann?" he had said. They were so close. The moon bathed the lake and poured down through the trees like soft velvet on them. "Ann. Ann . . ." Then he was kissing her.

How often she had replayed that night, the sound of her name on his lips, the feel of his arms. His passion! Her musing always stopped there. But not today as she sped to meet him. "You're so desirable," he had whispered. "I've wanted you. Let's just live tonight, Ann."

Suddenly a horn blast caused Ann to jerk the wheel and weave back and forth across the centerline while drivers honked behind.

"Oh my gosh!" How fast had she been driving? It seemed a long time to pull over and stop the car. Shaking out of control, she said, "You idiot!" The girls will scream and wail, "An accident!" And "Mom, you were on your way to meet another man!" She saw her husband heartbroken had her foolishness turned out differently. In the still car, she let the scenes unfold.

Pulling her wits together, Ann started the car and drove on, lecturing herself.

"Dear Bob, he cares so much. A one-woman guy, no philanderer. Not the most romantic man in the world, but we'll work on that."

She wondered what Mark knew about love. She had heard gossip in Atlanta. "One affair after another, his wife's a wreck, taken to drinking. Poor Alicia, she is a gorgeous girl. So lucky they don't have children."

Misgivings ran rampant as Ann pulled up in front of Sebastian's. Waiting for valet parking, she thought she needed to discover the depth of her feeling for Mark.

She walked into the spacious Romanesque lobby to meet his embracing gaze. They met with arms outstretched. For a long moment, they stood holding hands, as Ann concealed shocked recognition beneath little spurts of laughter.

The headwaiter led them to a secluded gold-leafed alcove draped in blue, and directed them to dark velveteen seats.

Ann tried in vain to conjure up bygone happiness, but she could not bring the old Mark into focus. He has gone to seed, she thought. Yet, when a pretty, young thing came to take cocktail orders, Mark evinced a familiar youthful spark. All through the meal, they rehashed events of the long ago summer.

Soon her brittle laughter punctuated their talk. She tried not to look at his thinning faded hair, round-rimmed glasses, and his paunch. Even a rakish, red-brown mustache added no pizzazz to this new Mark.

How sad, she thought, feeling her memories being seared.

Sebastian's put out a delectable fare, and she savored each course. Finally, with their plates cleared, she reached for his hand. "Mark, I've always needed to thank you for that wonderful summer. You were very special to me. And . . . I will let you in on a secret. I have fantasized about you all these years. Those memories helped me over the hard spots. It has been a real treat to share lunch with you, but I can't stay for dessert. I have to get home and make dessert for Bob and our girls." There is laundry to do and dinner to cook, she thought. "Thank you for a lovely visit."

Ann recovered her handbag from the seat, and standing, Mark tried to pull her into an embrace. She resisted, even as she took note of the odd expression on his face.

Waiting at the curbside for the car, she puzzled over that expression. Was Mark disappointed? She would never know, then, it came to her. She had seen that same expression when Mark tried to move farther than she wanted to go. A slight grin, as if he thought he would be luckier the next time. His game is so obvious. She could dispatch Mark's ghost forever.

The valet turned the car into the curb. Ann handed him a bill, got behind the wheel and drove away. Once she cleared traffic and headed down the rural Maryland highway, she reconciled herself to bittersweet memories of a long ago romance.

Bob. Dear Bob. We have weathered rough times before, she thought. We will plow on towards his retirement. Why, we will both still be young!

THREE WISE WOMEN

 AWN WAS YET TO BREAK when three women paused at an oasis several miles outside the gate to Bethlehem. Sliding from their burros to the sand surrounding a still pool, they held the donkeys' reins and stood waiting in the pre-dawn hour for them to drink. Melchidi, the eldest and wisest, flicked her reins. "Gaspidi, Balthazidi, hurry! Yon star moves ahead of us."

Looking up, Gaspidi shouted, "Oh no! The star no longer moves!" She tossed the end of her shawl-like head wrap, embroidered with gold thread, over her shoulder.

Pulling the bottom of her long royal blue mantle up above her knees, the wise leader put one foot in Gaspidi's cupped hands and slide sidewise onto her animal's back. She shouted, "Mount up, girls. We spent too much time with that putz, King Herod."

Melchidi glanced back to see Balthazidi hold cupped hands for their fellow traveler to mount. Melchidi and Gaspidi rode ahead, leaving Balthazidi to pull herself onto the burro's back as best she could. Soon the wisest of the three gave a backward glance at Balthazidi just as she jerked her white head wrap over her hair and secured the end over her shoulder. She had safely managed to side-seat her animal, and Melchidi grinned at her fellow traveler's puzzled leer.

The three women had traveled from the East by way of Jerusalem. There, they had inquired of the place where the King of Jews was born.

Herod, the king of Judea, had heard of the prophesied birth. He called forth the three wise women. "When did this star appear?" Without awaiting an answer, he had sent them on their way with an admonition to, "Go search out the child. When he's found return with word so I might go and worship him."

The women had followed the bright star to the oasis, a far distance. Now they must seek out the new babe before dawn took away their star.

Whipping their small beasts, they continued toward the bright light when a man on a camel approached them. Melchidi pulled one end of her long red scarf over her head and across her lower face. Sensible enough to ask directions rather than flounder around beneath a passing star, she said, "Do you see yon star hanging there? What place lies beneath it?"

After more questioning, he gave directions to a small inn.

Heeding his instructions, the three wise women cropped their donkeys into a trot.

Arriving at the inn, Melchidi covered her head and walked inside. Standing before the proprietor, she asked, "Where is this child recently born?"

"They're in the stable," he replied. "When they arrived, there was no room in the inn."

"You schmuck! Don't you know *that one* is the prophesied king of old?" Melchidi's patience with the uninformed innkeeper waned. "Where is this stable?"

She returned to her wise friends, and following the path as directed, she, Gaspidi and Balthazidi entered the animal stall.

There they found Baby Jesus wrapped in swaddling and lying in the manger. A robed and head-covered Mary sat on a milking stool near the converted feed trough. Joseph her husband held his rod and knelt on the other side of the makeshift bed. Melchidi thought the mother appeared tired but gazed on her baby in blissful adoration.

"Mary, Joseph, we're shepherdesses come to worship this blessed child. God made him known to us, and a star guided us from the East." Melchidi untied a bundle and placed it before Mary. "We've brought gifts. Here are diapers, olive oil, and talcum powder for baby rash."

Gaspidi dropped her bundle in front of Mary and knelt before her. "I bring gold and food."

Balthazidi placed her bundle at Mary's feet. "My gifts are brush sweepers to clean this place and myrrh for fragrance." She had mentioned to her wise friends that her sorcerer instinct about myrrh—the scented gum used to prepare bodies for burial—could mean Mary's son might die.

"Alas," she had said, "I wished to find a less foreboding gift, but myrrh fell in the cleanliness mode of the sweepers."

Melchidi had warned her not to mention her foreboding to Mary.

Now, with their gifts presented, Melchidi looked around the stable. "Joseph, will you grab a shovel and clean the dung from this place? I would like you to rid the manger of that stinking straw and replace it with fresh." Then, "Gaspidi, get off your knees, get that loaf of round bread from the bag on your beast and then make a pot of lentil soup. Otherwise, why bring food all this way?"

To the baby, Melchidi said, "I'll get these wet swaddlings off and in no time at all, I'll have you smelling as good as burning frankincense."

She picked up Baby Jesus. "I'm going to the water trough and bathe this poor infant."

Returning, she placed the baby in Balthazidi's arms.

Balthazidi cuddled the babe and asked, "Do you see the angel standing over this scene?"

Melchidi, a non-believer in sorcery, said she did not see any angel.

"Well, she is stunned into silence by three women coming in here from out of nowhere, and a bossy one called Melchidi taking charge. She is reaching beneath her halo-highlighted, long flowing hair and scratching her head. The angel is asking, 'How can I announce there will be peace on earth as long as a Melchidi and those of her ilk are alive?'"

"If there is an angel, I see she did nothing about the conditions under which this royal babe was born." Melchidi's long headscarf draped down her front, handicapping the tasks at hand. She flipped the end over her shoulder. "Balthazidi, stop imagining and take care of the baby."

She was content, listening to Balthazidi sing to the babe. When Baby Jesus fell asleep in her friend's arms, and she placed him in the newly laid manager, Melchidi sensed everything was going well. The stable now smelled of Gaspidi's lentil soup, and she sniffed the seasonings and tasted for doneness. "Will we eat soon?" she asked Gaspidi.

The wise cook nodded, and Melchidi smiled as she breezed around with Balthazidi's gifted brush sweeper, picking up straw and piling it in one place. "We must leave while there is still daylight. There may not be a star to guide us back East."

The three wise women huddled on the stable floor with Mary and Joseph, dipping pieces of bread in the rich red soup. Soon all were sated, and the three wise ones went to the trough to rinse the bowls. Balthazidi whispered, "I received this warning. We must not return to Herod but circumvent him by traveling through another land to our home."

"I have great respect for the king. Why must we avoid Herod?" Gaspidi wanted to know.

"Why can't we track back to Jerusalem?" she whined.

"Shush! Do you want them to hear?" Melchidi nodded toward the stable. "Herod is a putz, Gaspidi. He is up to no good." She sensed she had a notch up on the ring of wisdom when it came to her two shepherdess companions.

Balthazidi warned, "He will call us before himself again and pry into the whereabouts of the babe. We cannot give him the location. He plans to have all the male babies in Judea killed."

"Sounds like him," Melchidi said. "Don't you know he will not tolerate another king in the land?" She motioned for the other two to follow her and bid Mary and Joseph farewell.

Gathering up empty gift bags, Melchidi went to Mary. She placed a hand on her shoulder. "God be with you, new mother." She turned to Joseph. "I pray you will care for mother and child."

"May our Father in Heaven bless you," Mary waved from her stool.

Melchidi waited for Joseph, an humble appearing man, to acknowledge their departure. He had spoken not a word, and she wondered if that stunned look on his face meant anything. He lifted a limp hand to her and returned to whatever went on in his head.

Turning away, Melchidi noticed Balthazidi waving toward the head of the crib at nothing. Thinking her sorcerer friend waved at the imaginary angel, she shook her head and motioned for Balthazidi and Gaspidi to follow her out of the stable.

"Go mount your asses and let's be off."

Melchidi mounted quickly and waited for Gaspidi to mount from the side of the watering trough to her place on the donkey's back. She turned to see Balthazidi standing at the entrance to the stable and motioning to someone inside.

Joseph came to her side, and Melchidi overheard Balthazidi tell him she had a visit from her guide. "I had a vision of King Herod killing all the male babies. You must not return to Jerusalem."

Joseph raised his hand as though to stay her. "I know. An angel appeared in my dream and warned me of just such a happening. We will go to Egypt and abide there until Herod is no more."

Balthazidi left him and mounted her burro.

As they whipped their beasts and rode away side-by-side, Melchidi thought of the fine showing they had made. "Well, girls," she said from her mount, "we asked for directions, brought practical gifts, and cooked and cleaned. I am satisfied we fulfilled our mission in a wise manner."

Cropping their small animals, the three wise women rode on a route that would avoid Herod, the king. Circumventing Jerusalem, they came upon a caravan traveling in the opposite direction.

Pulling headwear over their faces, they inquired of news of the king. Told that indeed, Herod declared all male babies were to be killed, Gaspidi cried aloud. "How can I love my king if he kills babies?"

Melchidi reined her donkey close to Gaspidi's mount and reached for her hand. "Save your lamentations, dear. I said Herod is a putz. He is a tyrant."

The three wise women left the caravan and rode on to the oasis ahead where they and their animals could quench their thirsts. Melchidi dismounted and ran to Balthazidi. Embracing her, she said, "My wise friend, I believe you have an angel lodging in your head. Forgive me for doubting you. If I were so blessed . . ."

SEEKING CHRISTMAS JOY

"Oh, man," Jay complained, as he watched the last of the ginger cookies disappear.

Kate Wiley and her children arrived late for the church Christmas party. Jay and his younger sister, Jennie, rushed to join the other youngsters.

A Christmas tree trimmed in cutouts of biblical characters and wrapped in paper chains stood in the corner of the Sunday school room. Brother Chandler stood near the tree in Santa Claus garb fashioned by Mrs. Chandler. Jay fell in line with the boys walking past the minister. With a pat on the back, the minister handed each child a small gift, and said, "HO, HO, HO."

Kate scanned the faces around her. The party never changes, she thought. Year after year the same cookies, same punch, same little Bibles for gifts. It is always the same dry, unfeeling "Ho, Ho." Where is the spirit of Christmas? How can we bring joy to the season? It is more important than ever. Kate, a recent widow, thought about her children's first holiday without their father.

The next morning, Kate came downstairs in her robe and slippers to find Idella, her one-day-a-week housekeeper, and Georgia, the cook, with heads together and whispering.

"Miz Wiley, I left Gabe parked in his wheelchair at Jude's store. You know Jude. He's liable to walk out front and leave Gabe sitting there all by hisself." Idella's words came between heavy intakes of air, and she wiped her face with her print, bibbed apron. "I ain't got much time, but I wanted to tell you. Gabe's done ask a mill hand to cut a Christmas tree for you and the children." She drew a deep breath, gaining control of her speech. "Hack said he'll bring it on his truck. We don't want you to go out and buy a big old tree you be too tiny to wrestle with."

Idella's eyes lit up in her dark face. "Jest leave it to Gabe's timber man to pick out the prettiest, tallest tree he can find. Gabe told him it had to reach the ceiling."

"That's wonderful, Idella." Henry, her late husband, had always brought the tree home on Christmas Eve. Kate felt relieved of having to select a tree and all that getting it erected in the living room entailed.

Several days later, Christmas Eve morning greeted Kate with an overcast and cold temperature—an indoor-kind of day. Wrapping gifts behind her locked bedroom door, she imagined Jay and Jennie's happy faces when they unwrapped presents the next morning. Remembering they did not have a tree, she hoped Idella had not forgotten. It is too late to find one now, Kate thought. Suddenly, she heard a commotion below.

Descending the stairs, she saw Hack struggling to move a tall cedar through the front door. With great effort, he pulled the cross board stand through the threshold.

Idella and Georgia came through the doorway behind him.

"Show me where you want it, Miz Wiley." Hack wiped his brow with a handkerchief.

Kate, watching with her mouth agape, pointed to a window in the living room.

Soon the tree stood tall and erect in its place, and Idella straightened a large red ribbon tied to one branch. "Merry Christmas, Miz Wiley. It's our present to y'all. Mine, Gabe's, Georgia and Hack's too. We didn't know what else to get you."

Kate whispered, "It's a beautiful gift. Thank you." Tears welled, and wiping her eyes, she realized all the noise had brought the children running into the living room. She went to the storage area beneath the staircase and pulled out decorations.

Hack and the children circled the tree, draping red and green roping. Georgia placed tinsels on the branches, and Idella and Kate hung red and gold ornaments from past Wiley Christmases. Then, everyone stood back admiring the tree and Kate gasped as ten-year-old Jay climbed onto Hack's shoulders and hooked the gold foil star on the tiptop point.

"Will you look at that!" Georgia said.

The awe on her face pleased Kate, and she felt such pride as her son took on the role of star-hanger, the part his father had played on past holidays.

That evening after dinner and Georgia had left for home, Kate told her children that she had a surprise. "We're going out tonight to find Christmas joy."

Jay and Jennie helped load the Buick with gift baskets, and a beep of the horn announced their arrival at Georgia's house. At the door, Kate chimed, "Merry Christmas, Georgia! Merry Christmas, Hack. We have come in search of Christmas joy."

Georgia, still wearing her work apron, welcomed them into a room with a double bed, cast iron heater, cane-bottomed chairs and a low bench along one wall. A small pine, circled in popcorn roping, stood in the corner.

Hack picked up a *Sears, Roebuck Catalog* and scissors from the floor. "I was just about to cut out some pictures of toys to hang on the tree," he said. "How about you cut the pictures, Jay?" He reached for a ball of twine. "The rest of us, we'll thread them with this string, and Jennie can hang them on the tree."

As the last picture hung in place, Hack leaned back in his chair and laughed.

Kate heard the glee in his chuckle, and watched Georgia run off toward the kitchen.

She returned with a beribboned package and placed it beneath the tree. "Now Hack, don't you peek before tomorrow morning." She wagged a finger. "You the worst . . . just like a little kid."

The Wiley children giggled at her scolding, and Kate stood and placed a fruit basket under the tree. She suggested they sing a carol. "Who knows the words to *Noel*?"

All but Hack nodded that they knew the song.

Georgia hummed the key and Kate saw faces sober as they sang of the reason for their celebration.

The last note of the carol sounded, and Jay piped up. "Let's sing *Jingle Bells*."

"Yeah, *Jingle Bells*," Jennie begged.

Hack dropped his chair legs to the floor and directed the chorus. His jazzy rendition broke the tune into lyrical segments and gales of laughter from the others.

"Come," Kate said, motioning to everyone. "Let's go to Idella's and leave a holiday wish for Christmas joy with her and Gabe."

"Just a minute, Miz Wiley. I got presents for them." With beribboned gift bags in one hand, Georgia grabbed her wrap and waited for Hack to pull on his coat before they all ran for the car.

Gabe answered the door, and Idella stood behind his wheelchair.

Their cherub-like beams delighted Kate. She offered a green beribboned basket lined with dried magnolia leaves and filled with fruits, nuts and pinecones. "Our tree is beautiful, Gabe. Thanks so much to all of you for a thoughtful gift." She squeezed the hands of each one and hugged Idella and Georgia.

Nodding agreement, Georgia handed her presents to Idella and Miz Wiley. Both thanked her and Idella sniffed at her package. "It sho smells like your homemade cookies." Settled inside, Kate agreed with Idella that it must be the cookies Georgia gifted them with on special occasions.

Grinning pleasure, Georgia gave them a foxy look. "Like Hack, y'all will just have to wait."

"Well, what more can we do to make this a memorable Christmas? You can put us in the Christmas spirit, Idella, if you sing *Silent Night*."

In a twitter over the gifts, she said, "I sho will. Y'all got to help now." She caught the tune on a low hum and eased into the lyrics written about a wondrous and magical night.

Kate watched the faces in the room, as each experienced the carol in their own way. Georgia's eyes closed, and she hummed along. In the dimly lit room, Kate's children's eyes twinkled like stars, and she wiped away tears.

On the last note, Gabe and Hack shouted, "Hallelujah."

Happy echoes of "hallelujah" and "Merry Christmas" rebounded as the merrymakers shouted from the door.

Kate knew she had found Christmas joy.

COMING HOME

WAS THERE EVER ANYONE SO wretchedly lonely? Four days on the train, every seat filled. I had spoken to no one, or they to me. My mind dwelt with the tortured-of-the-damned. Those filling the seats could not be burdened with my misery, and I could not get beyond it.

A year had passed since I had left Alexa standing on the platform. She smiled through her tears and said she dreaded our separation. We did not know how long the separation would be. We would have married had I not volunteered for navy service.

"I loved you, Alexa!" I cried it aloud and wondered if anyone in the rail car heard me, vowing not to even entertain the thought of love.

The train had pulled me through hell on that homeward trip. Clickity clack. Clickity clack, a constant drumming on the rails, beating at my despair. Not even an occasional dull thud stopped the clickity clacking from sounding out, "You lost her." Those words pounded against my senses.

Vibrating, jarring, swaying . . . I had dreamed of happier times. Stolen embraces and kisses in the porch swing . . . against her father's wishes. We lingered at the door in a heated sway of bodies before our last goodnight kiss. Oh, Alexa! Why couldn't you wait? The words screamed in my head. Her flaming red hair, luscious strawberry-ripe lips, stacked curves in all the right places . . . All of it danced behind my closed eyes.

I had felt my emotions building beyond control, then, like a long awakening, I became aware of the train slowing. Glancing out the window,

I saw East Texas oil wells and trails leading out of town, trails where Joanie and I had ridden our horses.

Gathering up my gear, I headed to the rear of the car.

Without expectation in the way of a welcome home, I stepped down on the tarred apron and before I reached the station door, I heard someone calling, "Flash."

Only one person called me Flash. Joanie had said that Jackson, my real name, was too uppity. "Since you sail your horse Satchel across the ground like the speed of light," she said, "I tag you Flash."

I still liked the idea of her having a special name for me. Maybe we can be riding pals again, I thought as I left the train. My mind conjured up the image of her the day she came new to our third grade class. She was a real tomboy. In junior high school, we began riding horses together. What was her horse's name? Mistletoe. She could sit a horse with the best of them.

I remembered there was not much feminine about Joanie. Sunday was the only day she did not wear jeans, boots, and a cowgirl hat, and then she tolerated a dress just long enough for church service. She was not much of a looker. Hazel eyes, long blonde hair streaming down from her hat.

The day of my homecoming, I stood there on the station apron remembering her infectious laugh when the train spewed steam before moving away down the track. It jarred me out of my reverie and at the station entrance, again I heard "Flash."

This young thing came running up to me, all out of breath. Shiny hair curled around her smooth face. Her dress was some shade of greenish-blue that brought out the green in her eyes. A shoulder-strap bag and wedge sandals polished her image. I was looking at a real live lady.

"Hi, Flash. Welcome home. You don't recognize me, do you?"

Suddenly, the veil lifted. "Joanie?"

She put her arms around my neck and planted a strawberry kiss on my lips.

Dropping my duffel, I grabbed her into my embrace. Releasing her, I stammered, "Gosh darn, Joanie! You've . . . well, you have changed. Come on, let's get ice cream at Pistol Pete's."

Talk came easy and a miserable train ride faded from my mind like the sun sinking on the western horizon.

In the year after my homecoming, we met and talked real often, catching up with each other. Joanie made it easy for Alexa to fade into a nice memory, and on our wedding day, a bright spring sun lent itself to a Texas barbecue reception.

Just about everyone in town came for the occasion.

Now, five years later as I write this in my journal, two little sprouts run about our home. Well, one is a cowgirl and the other, a cowboy. Their names are Diane and Clarke.

Speaking of names, when you read this, I want you to know that your mother does not call me Flash anymore. She says it does not fit my successful and respectful businessman's persona.

Kids, it is late into the night and I sit here at my desk. My eyes feel tired as I try to come to the end of this entry, but I want you future grownup cowpokes to know how your mother reentered my life.

Occasionally, I pinch myself and remember what a fortunate man I am to have come home to a gorgeous grown-up lady.

THE BEST OF MICHELANGELO

MYRA BECKETT STOOD AMONG A tour group at the edge of Vatican Square. As the guide described the scene, a horse-drawn carriage clattered by, drowning out his voice. Myra looked from the mid-1600's colonnade to the obelisk, to the high windows of the Pope's apartment, then back to the curved colonnade. She stood in Rome, hardly believing her good fortune.

Drawing a deep satisfying sigh, Myra thought about her fantasy of such a time. She had dreamed it from the day she received a Fine Arts degree from the University of Illinois. So many things—a failed marriage, divorcee, a bout of depression before she could resume teaching—had delayed her dream. Over fifty years old and sensing a sinking feeling she knew so well, she had shared her dream with Bob Linken, curator of the Castle Art Museum.

She told him she had not made a recognizable impression on the world of art. While still confident of her skills as an artist, she did not feel she had reached her potential.

Myra suspected her skills were not the only reason Bob had recommended sponsorship of her art tour in Italy. Romantically linked for several years now, perhaps Bob thought she would be more inclined to say "yes" to his marriage proposals. Marriage did not work the first time for her, so why would she want to try a second time?

Standing there, thinking of how she happened to be in Rome, she sighed and made a determination to focus on making an impression on the art world. Heaven knows, she had never made much of an impression on any other world. Not one to dress to impress, her natural curls turned gray now, received no more care than a shampoo and brush through. What does Bob see in me? I must take more care in presenting myself. She felt a sting of conscious about Bob.

"Follow me." The stout guide recaptured her attention. He said the balustrade topping Bernini's Colonnade held representations of saints and martyrs carved by the sculptor's students. As the group strolled behind him, he encouraged them to admire, from their vantage point, the grandeur of the whole—St. Peter's Basilica, the dome, the Apostolic Palace and the fountains.

Taking it all in, Myra imagined the colonnade arms stretching out to all humanity, drawing her into a loving embrace. The image of an embrace lacked the essence of reality. Suddenly, she felt disappointed, or was the feeling a desire to be completely separate from any distraction that would keep her from absorbing the creation of every art object.

Most every Sunday for most of her life, Myra had gone to Mass. She had read that the cavern housed the Chair of Saint Peter, the Veil of St. Veronica and the head of St. Andrew. It also held a large piece of the crucifixion cross and the lance used to pierce Christ's side.

She walked among the tour group across the uneven stone square and stepped up to the basilica door. Crossing the threshold, morning turned to dimness. She peered into it, seeking a fount. Dipping her fingers, she made the sign of the cross and stood in the background feeling small and exposed. For a moment, the world seemed at a standstill, and she dwelt beyond a realm of reality scarcely knowing where to focus.

Returning to a living continuity around her, she basked in the reverent silence. Beneath the dome, she looked up, admiring Michelangelo's work at age seventy-two. A few paces away, his *Pieta* gazed down on her lifeless son lying across her lap. The Madonna appeared beyond tears, as though tears might wash away the truth of what she saw.

Myra read the plastic-encased blurb on the wall beside the *Pieta*. She had studied art all of her adult life, taught it for twenty-five years. Now, in the presence of such greatness, she realized she knew so little. "How could Michelangelo at twenty four, capture such passion in the *Pieta*? What can I expect at my age?"

Turning from her utterance, she caught the amused face of a stranger standing next to her.

Feeling the heat of blush, she moved beyond the man only to return to the statue when he walked away. Her muttering forgotten, she gazed with artistic wonder and questioned her own artistic ability. How can something be a lifelong passion, and yet I stand here feeling art may no longer be speaking to me?

Then, was that a voice . . . ? Yes, it was a voice. She heard it as clear as words could tell. There, it was again. "I spent the rest of my life trying to match that achievement," it said. "Trying to be worthy of it. It's the only work I ever signed."

Hearing full sentences, Myra, taken aback, looked for people about her. No one stood nearby. "Who said that?" Was she the only one to hear the voice? "Wow," she whispered, "Michel, you're in my head."

Trying to accept the voice emanating from the air as mere imagination, she watched foreign priests scurry about with little suitcases. Perhaps the cases contain vestments, she thought, and they search for altars from which to say masses. She felt stupid and wondered if she was losing it again. The police will be called, and they will haul me to the loony bin in this foreign country!

Frightened, Mrya eyed with suspicion those milling about.

"No need to feel stupid and fearful. I have spoken to many before you. They never told they heard me for the very reasons you are feeling right now. I have my doubts that you too, will tell that you spoke with Michelangelo."

"I . . . I—"

"Don't make excuses. I know too many excuses."

What is happening here? Despite uneasiness, and for reasons she could not fathom, Myra wanted to hear more. Then she realized the voice had quieted. Disappointed, she regained a sense of herself and stood there listening to the shuffle of feet on the marble floor. Then, just when she thought all was back to normal, she heard the voice again.

"Millions have seen *Pieta*. Millions more will see it." She welcomed a return of the unseen source of words. "Few share what they have seen. What do you see, Myra? What do you feel when you look at my piece of art?"

"Uh . . . I uh, I see a stone monument representing the human quest for excellence." Myra thought her spontaneous response sounded intelligent. Lost in a subject dear to her heart, she forgot about those around her.

"Hm-m," Michel said. "Surely you see something deeper than cold stone. Your feeling, girl! What are you thinking? Step back to your first thought, when you raised your eyes to her."

Yes. The pitiful, lifeless human body, and the mournful mother looking as beyond crying.

"Good. You are getting there. And? What does she see that won't allow her to cry?"

Again, Myra was aghast. He read her thoughts. "How do you—"

"Never mind. That is not important. What is important is that you go away from here and share what you have seen and felt. Share it with the millions who will never see my work. Now, tell me. What are you going to share with them? What is the deeper meaning behind my *Pieta*?"

She had never felt quite so inadequate as now in the presence of this renowned, inanimate personage. "Are you asking me for the deeper meaning of your work?"

"Yes. What does it say to you?"

Myra studied the work and waited for something to come to her. Then, "I see the Madonna as the people of the world. People mourning for their desecration of the goodness and beauty provided for them. Christ's body . . . to me, it represents the condition of the world."

Was she making any sense at all? Here she stood, in this most holy of shrines, thinking not of the hereafter, Heaven or Hell . . . No, her thoughts were worldly. That would never do back home in St. John's Holy Chapel.

"Not bad. Not bad at all." Michelangelo gave a smug little laugh. "I want those viewing the *Pieta* to seek their own meaning in the work. Sometimes they lock into what I intended when I put my greatest sensitivity into that carving." He sighed. "Most often, they see only the beauty in carved stone, or the compassion of a mother who lost a son."

Then he whispered, "It isn't necessary to tell we had this little talk." Then, softer still and fading, "Just share my work as you see . . ."

Myra stood immobile for what seemed like eons, waiting, wanting to hear more—more of the secret conversation she would hold forever. Or would she? Perhaps she would share with Bob. He, like Michel, would encourage her to pour more passion into her artistic creations.

Passion, that is what is missing!

Was the world ready for her visit with Michel? How could she share with other art lovers what he had taught her? She carried the question out into the sunlit square. It had to be through the creative passion in her artistic work. Walking back to the tour bus, she knew Bob would help her find a way to explain her unusual experience of the famed painter. Already she missed Bob. He would be at the airport awaiting her return.

She felt lighter knowing that. The load of doubt in her creative abilities had lifted. No more fits of depression would keep her from pouring every ounce of passion she felt into a piece of her work. Moreover, she would share with her art history students what the *Pieta* spoke to her.

Now, on to Florence, she thought.

HOSTING THE WEDDING

MARGARET MEADOWS' DAUGHTER LAUREN WROTE that she and Brad were ready to be married.

After their graduation from an East Coast university, Lauren and Brad had gone west for his Master's degree. They had been living as if married for the past year. Margaret read her daughter's letter again and for the umpteenth time, said, "Yep, it's a new age."

Then she entered into a dervish-like spin of activity. Between mother and daughter, the date for a garden ceremony at the Meadows' home was set. Invitations went out and RSVPs received. A wedding consultant and aide were hired. Tables, chairs, plates, glasses and a champagne fountain, all reserved.

Margaret turned to engaging a minister. "Yes," she answered the clergy on the other end of the line, "the groom is divorced!" Slamming down the phone, she picked up the Telephone Directory, declaring she would find someone to marry them. A youthful-sounding voice came over the phone. The Monotheistic priest said he would be happy to marry them. Without knowing what to expect, Margaret marked off one more task and muttered, "Now for the caterer."

Before she could engage a food provider, the groom's brother died close to the wedding date on the mailed invitations. Margaret reached everyone on the list, relating the cancellation because of a death in the family. She explained by phone or note about a new date and time.

The soon-to-be-wed couple came to the East Coast for the funeral. Margaret and Hal attended the funeral out of respect for Brad.

With a new wedding date set before Lauren and Brad returned westward to pick up loose ends, the invited guests were again informed. Most everything appeared ready when the couple arrived a few days prior to their special day.

Margaret picked up Grandma Meadows, a teetotaler from the South, at the airport a few days behind Lauren and Brad. The next day, she, Grandma and Lauren spent an afternoon at the bridal shop for gown fitting and selection of the bride's headdress.

"No veil," Lauren said, choosing a headband of flowers.

Less than happy with her daughter's choice, Margaret drove home in silence. She ran a red light, and Lauren screamed at her. Not a peep came from Grandma riding in the back seat.

At home, things grew touchy. Grandma asked, "Honey, how do you want me to cut these potatoes?" Before Margaret could answer, "Are you serving liquor at the reception?"

Without thinking, Margaret blurted, "Oh heck, Grandma, make the potatoes geometric, and yes, I invited Jesus to turn water into wine." She turned to Hal. "What hotel should I call to house Lauren's attendants?"

Hal stormed, "Don't go booking rooms and running up bills more than you already have."

Margaret prayed it would not rain on the wedding for Hal refused to rent canopies. "If it rains, everyone can go inside. When this dad-blasted wedding is over, I can just declare bankruptcy." Snatching up the newspaper, he headed for his easy chair, mumbling about fifteen minutes of "I do" promises.

Margaret wondered if Bellevue Asylum had a room for her. Thankful Lauren was not around to hear her dad grouching, she said, "Hal, people are flying from the West Coast. We must provide places for them. I'm calling for reservations."

Several days later rentals arrived, guests were accommodated, and clever hands adorned decks and gazebo with ribbons and containers of yellow wild flowers. Lauren liked wild flowers.

In the living room, Margaret and Lauren stood behind Hal, watching him rub the back of his neck in a studied manner, as if counting invisible dollar bills. Margaret nudged Lauren. "Tell him," she whispered.

"Daddy, the flowers didn't cost a dime."

"That's good thinking, honey. It's looking real pretty out there."

The string combo was due to arrive any minute to find its place. At the same time, Lauren's former music teacher was coming to practice the wedding march. "Come on, you two. Help me push the piano." Hal pointed, "You want it in front of that window opening onto the upper deck?"

What kind of question is that? Margaret thought. With noticeable irritation, she said, "Yes, Hal, we want the guests on the lawn to hear the music."

Next day, a sunlit beauty and birdsong graced the September morning on the East Coast. The young priest arrived in yellow robes and bearing an altar table. A photographer walked around taking snapshots. A brother each of the bride and groom ushered guests to their garden seats.

The groom and best man took their places with antsy glances in the direction of the stairs leading from the upper deck. The wedding march sounded with several grating notes, and Margaret cringed, recalling years of music lessons.

Grandma looked up at her with mouth skewed to one side, but Margaret did not acknowledge her facial comment about the missed notes. Her beautiful daughter floated down the grassy aisle on her father's arm. Then, as the ritual "I do's" became vows, a numbing tiredness beset the mother of the bride.

The priest placed a red dot in the middle of Lauren's forehead, and Margaret looked at Grandma, hoping she did not see it. However, no such luck. The ceremony ended, and Grandma leaned into Margaret. "Just who is he a priest for? I didn't know Catholics did that."

Margaret did not try to explain. She grabbed Grandma by the arm and headed for the receiving line forming at the front door.

One of the groom's friends introduced his daughter. Grandma uttered a guttural sound, and the hostess noticed a well-endowed young lady wore a white, see-through top and no bra. Margaret hyperventilated and left the receiving line. Returning in a few minutes, she saw guests still trailed up to the line. Doing a quick estimate of those already passed inside, she clamped a hand over her gaping mouth. Eighty invited! There must be at least a hundred people here. Dear God, please let there be enough food.

With the last handshake and introduction, she followed the last of the line inside. She found some dishes empty and only spoonfuls of content left in other containers. The wedding consultant whispered in her ear, "There's no more food, and the champagne fountain is clogged up."

Margaret saw her youngest son working over the fountain. "Brad's mother brought a Whiskey Sour mix and poured it in the fountain. Lemon pulp . . . Mom, don't go into hysterics!" He caught her arm. Reassuring, he added, "Brad has chests of cold beer in the garage."

Margaret recovered and found the consultant and her aide filling champagne glasses from the bottles. People ate from plates on their laps. They sat on the upper and lower decks in chairs set up for the ceremony. "Tables!" Margaret said under her breath. Hurrying to the garage, she saw the tables, folded and stacked just as left when delivered. Sighing, she told herself there was no need to worry now and returned to the deck to visit with the guests.

Hal stood in a cluster of men, and she heard his raucous "haw, haws" above the other chatter. The best man offered the toast, and Lauren and Brad radiated happiness as they cut the cake. Beer and champagne flowed, and even Grandma, the teetotaler, with wrinkled nose sipped from a glass of the sinful potion.

It was late afternoon when Brad tossed the garter to the gathered bachelors. Then, Lauren threw the bouquet, and the newlyweds departed.

Guests trickled away, and with the last goodbye, Margaret flopped in a recliner. "Grandma, Hal, you're on your own. There is no food left and I can't move another muscle."

"Don't worry about us, honey," Grandma said. "It was a beautiful day and a lovely wedding. Now, what do you want me to make for supper? Don't get up, now. I'll find something in the pantry."

Margaret did not intend to get up. She sat in a tired stupor, thinking how thankful she was to have only one daughter.

ED AND ETH ON THE ROAD AGAIN
FIRST DAY OUT

$\mathcal{E}$D PUSHED THE SPEEDOMETER ABOVE the limit, ripping through Interstate 30's commercial canyon between Benton and Little Rock. He griped all the way about repossessed prefabs and motor homes in fenced lots dotting the route. "Them RVs ain't nothing but road hogs." Then he shared a few choice words with Ethel about churches named Abundant Life and Word Aflame. "What's wrong with plain old First Baptist and United Methodist? Huh, Eth? Huh?"

Ethel listened, waiting for his next bit of palaver, her patience yet to wear thin. Beyond Little Rock, Ed had little to say about picked-over cotton acres. Stubbles in harvested rice fields didn't spark his run-on commentary either. But coming up on Wheatley, he pointed to soybeans laid out in yellow pallets under the October sun. "Pretty time to be traveling, ain't it, Eth?"

Ethel smiled. Digging in her purse for winged sunshades, she thought how the open road was Ed's favorite universe. Rolling through open country transformed him. He amused her even when she tired of his yakking and knew before he opened his mouth what would come out of it."

This morning, the thermometer read forty-eight degrees when Ed backed the cab-over camper from their driveway. Now, they were well underway on yet another road trip as the early fall temperature climbed.

Heading toward Memphis on I-40, a convertible with the top down passed them. The driver's hair danced about his head like an airborne kite in a speedy breeze.

"Was that a Cadillac?" Eth asked.

"Whatever it was, want to bet that bare-headed dude's a Texan?"

"Now Ed, I won't even ask why you say such things."

He laughed. "Ah, Eth, beings you're one of them, you know Texans have everything bigger and better than us Arkies." Eth did not want to pursue his dig into her native state, and Ed drove on in silence, then out of his mouth came, "Anyways, that dude didn't have dual exhausts. Bet he wished he had them. Ours sure impressed old Larry." Over his shoulder, he pointed toward the rear of the camper as though she did not know an exhaust pipe when she saw one.

Ethel sighed. She could predict what was coming next.

"Larry would get dual exhausts if he could squeeze money out of his old lady. Remember, he worked up a spread sheet showing Lily that if anything happened to him she could live in comfort till she was a hundred and fourteen years old."

Ethel nodded and let his overworked remarks pass. At the next exit, she read aloud with askance the road sign. "Parkin?" And farther on, "Earle?"

"Eth, you suppose Earle sparked a girl back there in Parkin?" The words barely left his mouth before he stomped on the brake. "Did you see that big sign? It said, 'Get your vasectomy reversed.' I tell you, Eth, that kind of surgery would be somewhat touchy."

Ethel wiped her "funny" tears, and reaching over, patted Ed's bare leg beneath his plain shorts. Then she remembered the fear his braking on an interstate caused her. "Ed, please don't hit the brake like that again. You want to get us rear-ended?"

"Well, I can tell you right now, Eth, a rear-ender would be better than a reversed front."

Convulsing in snorts of laughter over her seatbelt, she wiped more tears, and noticed the pleasure her amusement brought to Ed's face. *What would I do without my old motor mouth?*

She settled back to enjoy the landscape, when suddenly she saw a sign. "Cracker Barrel! Watch for the exit, Ed. The sign said, 'Three squares in six miles.' When we get on I-55, the road won't have much to offer."

Ed nodded, but at eighty miles an hour, he zipped right past the exit to Cracker Barrel.

"Well now you've done it! It'll be miles before we eat."

"Ah, Eth, there'll be other places."

"Famous last words." She whipped out the road atlas, retrieved eatery brochures collected from other trips, and tallied distances.

While she added, Ed complained. "Have you seen any bumper stickers, Eth? Ain't nobody got a sense of humor anymore. You just don't see bumper stickers like you used to."

She looked up from the map. "We're twenty-something miles from West Memphis. I don't know about bumper stickers, but I am weary of the bumping and jarring. Take the other lane."

He glanced in the side mirror and whipped into the fast lane.

"Did you check the blind spot? You will get us killed, yet, Ed Corney."

"Do you hear them 'thump thumps' anymore? Suppose we're dead?" He lifted his baseball cap, cut a smile at her, and slapped it back on his baldness. He reminded her of their trip across the top tier states. "Remember that bumper sticker, 'If it ain't fun, why do it?' And the billboard that said, 'Jesus is watching you.' Across the road, one said, 'Adult Video, Super Stud.'"

"I can't remember all those silly things, but I do remember you acted like a super stud when you played 'chicken' with a Honda SUV. You scared me out of my skin. It's a wonder that we are still among the living."

Ed said that was some thrill, but he was missing the bumper stickers. "I guess we'll just have to look for more funny billboards. Look, Eth, wide open country! Now where in the rest of the whole, wide world you gonna find this?"

"Big deal. It's flatter than a fritter in the Arkansas delta." She pulled one blue jeaned leg up on the seat and rested back in the corner of the cab. Behind her sunshades, she eyed him through squinted eyes.

"I'd make a big deal over a funny bumper sticker if we saw one." Ed doffed his cap again, and turned a questioning glance her way. "I hope you're not going to sleep—Uh oh. Lookey over yonder! There it is, 'Adult Super Store.' Suppose we can get eats?"

"You'll eat there by yourself, Ed Corney. If you didn't drive so fast . . . oh, there! 'Skinny's 24-Hour Diner.'" Ethel pointed to the advertisement.

"Come on, sugga. Skinny can't fill this," he said, patting his oversized stomach as they approached the exit to I-55. "A ways back the sign said,

'Monitor your health daily.' I just monitored, and the meter read, 'Empty. Darn near starvation.'"

Ethel giggled. "You old fool." She straightened up from her slump in the cab corner and placed a hand on his shoulder. "You can forget Adult Super stores. We aren't stopping. Slow down," she yelled. "You keep passing McDonald's! There goes Pizza Hut. Wendy's ahead!"

Ed whipped the camper-truck onto the exit ramp, followed the eatery direction into the left lane and stopped at the traffic light. He made the turn and eased along in the right lane as Ethel searched ahead, right and left of the street, for the sign announcing Wendy's.

"There," she pointed, "on the right."

Inside the restaurant, Ed gave their petite server with a soft Tennessee brogue a dose of tomfoolery, and she kept their glasses filled with ice and sweet tea. Every few minutes, she stopped at the table to ask if they needed more tea, or if "everything was all right."

Their meal finished and waiting for the check, Ethel said, "You charmed her, Ed; now, what kind of tip are you leaving her?"

"Well, my tank's full of burger and fries. Guess a dollar will do."

On the road again, Ethel shook her head at his high-mindedness.

Soon, her husband called attention to bugs splatting on the windshield, interrupting the pleasure she gained from the autumn colors. "What did one moron bug say to the other? Huh, Eth? What do you think it said?"

"I don't know, but you're going to tell me."

"That bug said, 'It takes guts to do that.'" She giggled, and Ed swerved to avoid road kill. "Oops. I bet that coon said, 'It's murder to be caught dead on this road.'"

"You think you're clever, don't you?" Despite herself, Ethel laughed.

"Well, there ain't many billboards, and no bumper stickers. I've got to get my kicks, and there ain't no Route 66. Would you looky there? We are back in billboard land. There is a whole patch of them. Tomorrow, I will have one of them 24-four ounce, hundred percent, Angus beefsteaks.

Ed drove on for a few minutes without uttering a word. Ethel guessed he was savoring an imaginary steak. She gave him a quick glance, and he must have seen it and been jarred out of his trance. "Hey, Eth, how about turning on some Blue Grass and singing along with me?"

She switched on the radio, and they rode along singing, "Carolina moon keeps on a crying for your Carolina morning memory."

At nine o'clock that night, Ed drove under a service station canopy somewhere in Kentucky. Cutting the engine, he unfolded from the cab and stepped inside to ask permission to park for the night beneath a pole lamp beside the station.

He will do anything to keep from paying an overnight campground fee, Ethel thought. Oh, what the heck? He is my corny man, and he managed not to kill us on the first day out.

STASH THE KIDS, HONEY

"ELLO." JACK, HALFWAY ACROSS THE country and in a half-awake stupor, answered her ring.

"Hi, honey." Janet whispered into the phone. "How are you?"

Jack made an issue of his yawn and said he did not know. His gaping yawn travelled across the line like a communicable disease, causing Janet to yawn too. "What time is it?" Unmistakable irritation came through his voice.

"I'm sorry it's late, but there was no way I could call before now." Janet explained that her parents probably heard her from the next bedroom, and the squeaky stairs kept her from going to the other phone. She plumped her pillow, making herself comfortable on the bed. "I want to warn you, Jack." Janet hesitated and played with a button on her pajamas. "Honey, Mom and Dad are coming home with me. There are things you must do before we arrive."

"Like what?" Jack's response sounded of half-interest, then, "Did you say your *mom and dad?*" The "Oh, hell!" in his question came through loud and clear to her end of the line.

"Yes, Jack, Mom and Dad!" While Janet held somewhat the same feeling, she did not appreciate her husband expressing it in such an imagined expletive. She could not dwell on his attitude for time grew short. "Please, Jack, listen. They plan to stay a week. Honey, find a place to stash the kids. Tell them they can hide out in the attic . . . or in the basement. Stash them any place where they aren't seen or heard for a week."

Awake at last, her husband laughed at her silliness and reminded her of their conversation about just such an inevitable occurrence.

I am glad he remembers, Janet thought. How are we going to deal with this generation gap? She envisioned a wide spread between her conservative parents and their three teenage sons with long stringy hair and a teenage daughter in miniskirts.

Her parents did not approve of "hippies drinking beer and smoking cigarettes, to say nothing of pot." She could just imagine what they would say when they saw Moll in a short skirt.

Over the years, Jack Snyder's career had moved the family about the country and even to other continents. The grandparents saw their only grandchildren when the Snyders made an annual trip to visit. Or vice versa, never more than twice a year, leaving little time for grandparents to bond with grandchildren. Jack had tried to explain to Janet's parents the advantages the children gained from exposure to various locales and cultures.

Janet had added, "It broadens our viewpoints, and the children are learning to adapt and prepare themselves for life's many ups and downs."

With those lines of thought, Jack and Janet granted their offspring reasonable leeway to grow as individuals, to express opinions, and with their urging to accept the opinions of others. They allowed them to have private time, and with good judgment to choose their own friends.

Lying there on the bed in her parents' home, the problem of all the family cars popped into Janet's head. Counting the family sedan, there were four cars parked on the street. "Jack, Dad will be impressed that Mac earned money in summer construction to buy his used car to commute to the university. And that Molly worked at Burger King to buy your old Toyota so she could get to classes, but he's going to have something to say about all the cars."

She heard her voice rising, changed the phone to her other ear and cupped the mouthpiece in her hand. "Honey, Dad will notice that Jim drives a carload of neighborhood kids to high school, and even if it is in your carpool car, he'll say they ought to walk to school."

She sighed and thanked the Above that Bud was not old enough to drive.

Janet had to admit the difficulty of finding a parking space on Waterford Street. "I can hear Dad now." She tried to imitate his voice and words. "He will say, 'The idea of every kid having a car. It's ridiculous. Why, I walked a mile to a one-room schoolhouse.'"

Jack's broken laughter carried over the phone.

"Laugh if you want. How many times do you think I heard that broken record when I grew up in this house?"

"We all heard it, Janet. What do you think we will say when we have grandkids?"

"Ple-ease. Let's hope we don't live in the past." She fell back into her worry mode. "Dad will find it necessary to say something directly to the kids about the cars. He will tell them it is ridiculous to have cars at their age." Visualizing the look that was sure to pass between Mac and Moll, she knew their looks would not slip by her observant father.

Suddenly she blurted, "Oh my word, Jack! What are we going to do about the music?" Janet had learned to tune out Elvis' rock and roll, the Beach Boys' band, and Chubby Checkers belting out *Let's do the Twist*. This and more blared from hi-fis in three bedrooms all at the same time.

"How about we ask the kids to keep their bedroom doors closed and go to their friends' houses to listen to their music?"

Jack sounded wide-awake now. She told him that his suggestion may be a solution to the music problem, but there were so many more.

"You can bet if the kids leave the house during my parent's stay . . . well just guess what Mom will say? Especially Mom. 'Do the kids not want to visit with us? We rode all this way to see them, and they aren't grateful enough to stay here and visit with us.' Oh gosh, Jack, what are we going to do about the beer, the wine and liquor? You know they think we are a bunch of booze heads. Get it out of the fridge, take it to the basement and hide it out of sight."

By now, Janet's voice was a couple of decibels above normal. Suddenly, she realized it carried through the walls, and she whispered, "I don't know what you can do with the dry sink. Hide the booze and take an axe to the cabinet."

Hearing her husband's snorts, she visualized him bent over the bedside, gasping with laughter. It always amazed her that he found her dead-serious issues so funny. Jack's laid-back attitude was not much help in surviving their teenagers' stages. Here they were, facing a mom-and-dad visit that would surely play out just as she imagined it.

"Jack," she whispered into the phone, "stop laughing and listen. Do you think you can talk the boys into getting haircuts tomorrow?" She thought for a moment, then, "And tell Moll to pull out some decent skirts to wear while they're with us. Now listen, you are going to have to explain to them that it is only for a week, and they can do it for Grandma and

Grandpa. Tell them how much their grandparents like to brag on them. How much they love them."

"Janet, how much luck do you think I'm going to have? Your mom and dad are going to believe what they want to believe."

"Egad, Jack! Do something! Tell the kids their grandparents will be shocked to see those posters pinned all over their walls. Be sure their bedroom doors *are* closed."

Jack told her to calm down, that her parents' visit would be what it was.

"That's what I fear, Jack." She hit her pillow with a fist. "Listen up, call the Beslers in Australia and ask them to stash four teenagers for a couple of weeks."

Jack laughed and asked if she kidded.

"What do you think?" she whispered.

Janet cradled the phone, lay back on the bed with eyes on the ceiling as scenarios of the next two weeks played in her head. "Honey, the three of us will see you in a couple of days. When all else fails, pray."

Two days later, Grandma, Grandpa and Janet arrived. She noted one car parked in front of the house on Waterford Street. Turning into the driveway, Janet saw Jack and the four kids running out the door to greet them. The boys had haircuts, and Moll wore a dress down to her knees.

Inside, the dry sink sat disguised beneath a pretty cloth with a scented candle resting atop of it.

The next day, Janet heard Golden Oldies coming from one of the hi-fis. She stepped to the door of Mac's bedroom. Grandma danced with Mac, and Grandpa had Moll cutting a rug. Jim and Bud sat on Mac's bed, laughing at the whole scene.

Janet backed away from the door and walked down the hall to her bedroom. Sitting on the bedside, she was relieved that Mac's walls were stripped bare of posters. Our visit is going well, she thought. Pulling her legs and feet up on the bed, she rested back against the shams and gave some thought to outings with her parents.

Her mind wandered through any number of possibilities for entertaining them, but uppermost in her thoughts was finding a way to thank her terrific husband and children for saving Grandma and Grandpa's visit.

AW, SHUCKS

Creative Non-Fiction, Essays and Features

A COOKED GOOSE

*I*T WAS NOT DAD'S INTENTION to cause a problem when President Roosevelt proclaimed the last November Thursday in 1938 as Thanksgiving Day. Nevertheless, he set the stage for the drama, and it became an oft-told story woven into our oral family history.

Dad, a wiry little Irish descendant, flashed an impish twinkle in light blue eyes. Mom presented a more serious side. Later, listening to Dad relate the story, it appeared she did not think the day Gandy Goose met his fate was funny. As for my brother Frank and me, our sympathy favored Mom and Gandy. Only when we grew to appreciate Dad's nature, could we laugh with him and see the humor in the event.

He may have kept the memory alive during his lifetime, but even today the minuscule details of that holiday unreel before my eyes like yesterday's movie.

It began shortly after the proclamation. We watched Dad drive our gray Plymouth sedan into the detached garage behind the house. With headlights burning, he scrambled around the garage as if looking for something. Turns out, he searched for a coop to cage a tame white goose.

Dad entered the house with a beam of excitement and pecked Mom on the check. "Sorry I'm late, hon. I went to Buckner to buy a goose from old man Meinor. Now, talk about a real Thanksgiving bird, goose is the best. We'll have him fattened by Thanksgiving."

I doubt we had ever seen a real live goose. "Wow!" Frank said.

I was thrilled to have two pets—Poochie, our dog, and now a goose. My excitement bubbled over any connection between "Thanksgiving bird" and Thanksgiving table.

It was not until Dad got a kick out of telling the story that we learned what our parents said to each other after we were in bed that night.

In his narration, he told that my mother Annie said she had never cooked a goose. Dad told her to do it just as she would a chicken. "Roast it . . . just like my aunt did. I can taste it now . . . Aunt Venie's roasted goose. She said, 'But I never saw her cook a goose, Toby.'" Dad always related that at age eleven, he went to live with his aunt after a train accident took his mother's life. "Her culinary magic left an indelible impression on me," he told anyone listening.

The "fattening" days followed that night, and Mom did not seem too happy with Dad's surprise. Frank and I decided on a name for our new pet, with help from neighborhood kids. After school, we poked sticks through the wire coop, and Gandy pecked at them and hissed at us.

On Tuesday afternoon before Thanksgiving, clearly by accident, Frank set Gandy free.

Mom went into a fit. She brought out the whole neighborhood to help catch the bird. Round and round the Methodist churchyard went the chase. Gandy lifted off only to land in a different corner of the grounds, until at last someone managed to nab him.

"It's an omen. Why else would that white bird alight like an angel on sacred ground?"

We did not have an answer for Mom's question.

On Wednesday before Thanksgiving Day, school dismissed for the holiday through the weekend. Frank and I made our way home from school beneath a solid overcast of high, gray clouds. Looking up at the blanketed sky, I said, "I hope it snows six-feet-deep so we won't have to go back to school."

Four years younger than I, Frank echoed his agreement with a "Me, too."

Knowing that snow might fall once a year in southwest Arkansas, I did not expect much to come of my wish.

Skipping up the driveway, happy to be out of school if only for a couple of days, I anticipated Mom's after-school treat. Yeasty, home-baked buns, buttered and warm, or tasty teacakes, and there might be a cup of hot chocolate too.

Instead of treats, we found our cozy home empty. Mom was always there when we arrived from school. Where was she? Only echoes answered our calls.

Whether there to tell us, or not, Mom had trained us well. We changed clothes before a treat or any other activity. Dressed in play clothing and without a treat to salivate over, we headed outside to Gandy's backyard coop to give him our after-school attention.

We continued calling out to Mom, and standing there beside Gandy's empty coop, we pondered the mystery of his disappearance. Little did we know that despite omen or angel, on Thanksgiving Eve, Mom had called on a young neighbor boy to decapitate our pet goose.

We kept calling, and soon a weak response came from the direction of an old barn about a football field's length from the back of our house. We found her there, standing at the back fence of a cow lot. On the ground beside her was a bucket of water emitting a wisp of vapor. Looking across the fence, I was sure snow had fallen. It soon became clear that it was not snow at all. White feathers had drifted across the bleak field to clump around the corn stubbles.

Mom sobbed and picked at a pitiful looking fowl. We stared in amazement as she shoved a nude goose at us and tried between sobs to explain. "I-I can't get the down of-f. I-It's stuck all over the skin-n." She wiped her eyes on a well-worn brown sweater sleeve. "I've been picking this goose since three o'clock. Your daddy will be home soon."

We stood there, cold and crying with her as the snow-like clouds disappeared in the dusk.

Then, Frank heard Dad drive into the garage and ran to tell him where we were.

Holding a flashlight, Dad walked up and stood for a moment, staring at the sorry state of affairs. All three of us tried to explain.

To our consternation, our dad burst out laughing. "I thought you had all the instructions you needed, Annie."

His laughter and comment brought Mom to a stance. She stood silent in her drab cotton dress and long cotton stockings. Wisps of dark auburn hair escaped thick braids crisscrossed above her nape. The de-feathered, gray-skinned bird dangled from one hand. With eyes set on Dad, in one swift move, she kicked over the bucket of water, unleashing an odor of wet feathers.

Right away, Dad sobered. "I forgot to tell you, Annie. You don't dip a goose in hot water like you do a chicken. A goose is picked dry. You've got a mess if the down sticks to the skin."

"O-oh." Mom wailed, holding out the mess she had made.

Sensing her raw feelings, Dad approached with caution. Reaching out, he pulled the goose from her hand. "Come on, honey. Let's finish up inside."

As that Thanksgiving season passed into future years, I forgot how they managed to remove the goose down. I have even forgotten how the bird tasted. If it was anything like the wild duck Mom cooked, I know why we never had goose again.

The thing is, messy down and roasted goose flavor were not the important pieces of the memorable event. Important was Dad's attempt to recreate a part of his youth, Mom's effort to make it happen, and Dad's storytelling, which wove such threads into our family tapestry.

GOING TO PIGGOTT

AST LITTLE ROCK, JACKSONVILLE AND Cabot, the dual highway stretches northward in a line of curving pavement framed in Queen Anne's lace. On either side of the byway, small towns lie in the distance, too far away from our traveled route to see. Hardwood foliage and blooming Mimosa trees present the freshness of summer.

Our starting point began this morning among tall Ouachita Forest pines. On reaching groves of hardwoods, appearing as though a gardener had used a hedge trimmer to level all their tops to one height, I ask, "Why do those trees not grow taller?"

"More than likely, the roots reached a granite surface," my husband says.

I ponder a question for the Forestry Service while admiring the symmetry of open land and trees. Soon knee-high corn—some shoulder-high, depending on planting times—crops up in varied shades of green fields. I turn to my husband. "It's comforting to see that grain will fill America's bread basket this winter and ethanol will help fuel our transportation systems."

"Yeah," he says.

Suddenly, the landscape turns into miles and miles of flat delta. We are in God's country. Most of the many roadside churches announce their Baptist faithful. It's Sunday, but the farmers are taking no mind of it. Dust stirs from tractors disk-ing the soil. It sweeps across our path or swirls off in the distance. "Those farmers must think it's a weekday."

Husband glances at me with a frown. "God understands timing is everything to a farmer. They plant and till when the time's right and the climate permits."

"Oh, I know." Rolling my eyes at his obvious response, I am drawn to acres and acres of carpet laid out on both sides of the road. It is a dazzling green view of tender rice shoots springing up between dirt levee-ed canals serpentining through the fields. Again, comfort flows down to the pit of my stomach. We can depend on our Arkansas farmers for food.

Suddenly, the road noise changes from the "blump, blump, blump" of concrete dividers to the smooth sound of new pavement and the "purr, purr, purr" of the car's engine. All is well until we arrive at that "hellish" stop sign where new pavement ends and I ease toward the moment of decision.

"Left to Walnut Ridge. Right goes to Jonesboro," my navigator says.

Of course, I know right goes to Jonesboro. Just a tad irritated, I say, "Yes, the sign tells me that." In all the years of going to Piggott, it never changes. On every annual trip, logic dictates that I go eastward at this intersection. So, I move into the right yield lane.

Before I can make the right turn, hubby raises his voice. "You know you weren't supposed to go to Jonesboro! I've been talking about Walnut Ridge all the way up here!"

This place lends itself to the near clubbing of my travel mate. Headed toward Jonesboro, I seethe, more angry with myself than he for making the same mistake at the same place year after year. Slowing the car, I see in the rear view mirror that a truck rides my bumper.

Husband scouts ahead for a turn-around. Soon I make a quick spin-off onto a gravel entry to a business, and we bump around the parking lot and back upon the highway.

Now heading westward, we travel a few miles toward Walnut Ridge before curving back eastward. I wonder who in road engineering can explain this backward maneuver to me.

We ride on, silence filling the space between us, as I anticipate the mystery of Crowley's Ridge. This elongated barrier, formed ages ago, rises up suddenly from the flat land. Did the New Madrid earthquake realign the Mississippi River and push up the sandy soil that forms the ridge? I had read that Ice Age glaciers may have formed it, and that today, it protects an area beyond the river from flooding.

On an elevator ride across the ridge's rolling hills, suddenly we drop down into the inviting little town of Piggott—a quaint village of active people, antique and novelty shops, and lest I forget, The Diner. Piggott is best known for the Hemingway-Pfeiffer Museum and Educational Center, and the Barn Studio where Ernest wrote parts of *A Farewell To Arms* and various short stories.

Reaching the business zone, we park in front of the Downtown Inn where we lodge for the week. George Forest and his wife Lou own the inn.

I am in Piggott for another weeklong creative writers' retreat and Deanna Dismukes' retirement party. Deanna is retiring as the museum's educational coordinator. Beginning tomorrow in the Education Center, Rob Lamm, a professor at Arkansas State University, will mentor attending writers. Roland Mann mentors the fall retreat.

For a number of years, my attendance holds steady, and once again I find it all worthwhile.

While I gain stimulation for a new writing project, my husband plays golf at the Sugar Creek Country Club. Or, he hangs out in the hobby store where he and George share war stories, drink coffee, or sip a malt from the old-time soda fountain.

At week's end, after renewing staff and fellow scribe friendships, I leave Piggott eager to begin a new book. Once again my writing pals give validation of my sanity. They too express confusion about that same highway change, eastward to Jonesboro or west to Walnut Ridge. On every return trip from Piggott, at the same juncture, both my husband and I find the road sign directing us to Little Rock a challenge.

However, the nick in the road will not keep us from going to Piggott.

ATTENTION, PLEASE!

"MARRIAGE IS NO PRIMROSE PATH." A truer statement might never be made.

Marriage is like a flight through turbulent air—fast, with lots of jars, and ups and downs. Everyone who has been or is married knows this.

I have a suggestion for making the institution of marriage better. Turn ups-and-downs on end, so that they become downs-into-ups. Now keep in mind, I have only my own case study to back up my theory, but surely others out there can support it.

Wedding days seldom come off without a hitch. Hitched, yes, but I mean without something going haywire before, during or after the ceremony to foreshadow what a couple has taken on. Nothing traumatic, mind you, but hints and perhaps needling little incidents.

Take my wedding day, for instance. I thought a prince had found his princess, the one that fit the shoe. Before our ceremony, I believed we were going to be happy ever after. Clues about the future did not appear on my scope. If there were any, I failed to store them. Oh, there was a bit of foot-dragging on the day, but I, like most brides and grooms, got through the fear factor.

Then it happened. Past the foot-dragging, the "I dos," and on the road to the university, several incidents caused my theory to form. The first was a flat tire on the old Blue Bomber, the car my groom's parents gave to us newlyweds. With the tire repaired and on our way out of town, the car's headlights failed. It was too late to have the lights fixed, and we headed for a hotel I had sworn would not house me on my wedding night.

Were these foreshadows of our future?

I must have stored these and other such incidents to bring up later. When we had a spat, my groom accused, "You always bring up the past. Let it go." Perhaps he was right. From my experience, one should recall all the infrequent little wisps of pleasure and brush those foreshadows away until married for a while.

Can it be that easy to turn a downer into an upper?

After an anniversary day completes the first blissful year, a bride discovers her man is not nearly as talkative as when they dated. He does not ask her out for dinner or take her to the movies. Evenings are spent on the couch watching TV, and the couple uttering not a word between them.

Now, I am thinking this is the moment—right now—to turn a downer into an upper.

The bride must gently grapple the remote control from his hands and say, "*True Grit* is showing at the Malco tonight. Let's go." She can expect a struggle gaining a hold on the remote. He will have all kinds of excuses for not going out, but a wife must be strong.

It just might work, but if it doesn't . . . well, the next evening she should be dressed in the sexiest little dress in her closet, and her hair arranged in an up-sweep that invites a kiss on the neck. High heels on the feet and an evening bag swung on her shoulder, she says, "I'm going to Tranquillo's for dinner, honey. You feel up to coming?"

Okay, you say you know what your husband will do, and it is not pleasant. Do you know?

My theory is it does no harm to try.

If over the years you've tried, and the marriage creeps toward the beyond, and you still haven't been able to turn downers into uppers, then it's time to try this. Wrap your body in Saran Wrap and greet him at the door. I guarantee he will have you upstairs in the bedroom so fast your head will swim. On second thought, Saran Wrap might be a bit too revealing. A little black bodice, a garter belt and black stockings can disguise some of the fat rolls but not the cellulose.

If you are lucky, his eyes will flick from a feather plume in the hair right down to stiletto heels on the low end.

I'm thinking this just might work.

Well, maybe not. I know what my husband would do. He would gaze at me as though thinking I had lost my last crackers, then say, "Put away the fan, Lola, and make my dinner."

If you have made it to this point, my theoretic conclusion is you are right back to the couch-sitting. Not really, for now, each of you has a recliner and you are happy to let the TV talk.

Should all your tries fail, then have kids. I can guarantee you will not have to try for romance again for a long, long time. The problem will turn into one that no longer allows that consideration.

BODY TALK

I TURNED THE PAGE ON FIFTY and suddenly found myself on the shady side of the hill.

Despite the shady spots, I told myself, I must not give up the effort to bring in the sunshine. And the fun. But even with care and attention, I noticed the years tripping over each other on the race from eighty to eighty-one, then eighty-two.

At the eighty milestone, the old bones, skin and sinew began chattering at me. Two years later, it was more than chatter. More like nagging control.

Now, I get up in the morning with a thought to doing my stretches. Stretching is about all I can muster anymore in the way of exercising. "Uh uh!" Gasping for breath, the body says, "I didn't sleep a wink last night. Sit me down in my easy chair."

"No," I say. "Instead, I'll just take a short walk."

"You mean you're going to take me out on a hot day like this? I can't believe you would do that to me at my age."

I tell myself to forget the exercises and the walk and just take a shower.

In the bathroom, Old Bod warns, "Be careful in here. Watch that step-over into the shower, and don't rub my blue spots too hard. They will just spread into more and bigger black bruises."

Having successfully maneuvered the shower and minded the bruises, I dress and remove the vacuum cleaner from the closet. It takes about an hour to clean the floors. I think about undertaking the dusting, but decide to postpone that task and head for the recliner.

"At last you're wising up," Old Bod says, as I collapse back on the chair.

After a fifteen-minute rest, I remember I must make a run to Wal-Mart. In the parking lot, I dislodge myself from the car—no small feat in itself—and the body sounds off immediately.

"Slow down, now. Don't walk so fast. Watch your step! I don't need any broken bones when you fall." Old Bod has already reached the conclusion that a fall and broken bones are in my future.

Back at the car after two hours of walking the store aisles, I bring my body home and put away the groceries. "I'm pooped," it says. "Take me to the chair. I can't make it through any more activity today." Stressing every ache and pain imaginable, it clearly demonstrates who is in charge.

So, resting on Old Bod's throne with swollen legs and feet elevated, I dose off.

Suddenly, time has elapsed and an in-head alarm goes off. With a start, I leap from the chair.

"Hey," Bod screams. "Watch it. My head's in a spin. Are you deliberately trying to kill me?"

"It's past time to start dinner," I say. "He will be home from the golf course any minute now. He'll be hungry."

"To heck with him," Bod says. "Let him make his own meal."

Well, what do you know? I think that is the best advice I have had all day. But do I heed Old Bod's advice? No. I head for the kitchen to make my golfer a decent meal.

At the end of the day, Old Bod stops complaining to relish a nourishing meal and take a long rest on the recliner before bedtime.

AH, THE AROMA

WHATEVER POSSESSED OUR NEIGHBOR TO ask my ten-year-old brother to go with him on a wild duck hunt? Whatever possessed my mother to allow it? Dad did not hunt. Frank had never held a gun, but off he went with a friend on a dark, damp Arkansas day to some watery area.

No one in Mom's family engaged in the sport. "We don't even own a gun," she said. "If your daddy even suggested we have a gun in this house, I would disagree." She fretted as the day wore on, and second-guessed, saying she should not have allowed Frank to go off with someone carrying a gun. "If your daddy had been here, he wouldn't have permitted him to go hunting. What if there is an accident? What if . . ." She apparently found it too difficult to express the unfinished thought.

When Dad was not home, Mom had a tendency to conjure up the worst.

Standing over the ironing board, she moved the flat iron in a nervous fury over wrinkles. She slammed the iron on end to readjust garments and attack other creases. From this chore, she found more and more tasks to take up the time.

Mom was in a frenzied state by late afternoon when Frank returned. If she saw the dressed fowl in his hand, she did not acknowledge it. Grabbing him up in an embrace, her worry frowns disappeared in laughter.

As she released him, Frank grinned up at her and held out the dead duck as though it were a prized trophy. "Look, Mom, Mr. Lewis didn't want it. He said you could cook it."

"Oh my gosh!" she uttered and rubbed her forehead, and I thought she was trying hard not to put a damper on Frank's gift. "Wild things have a . . . a wild taste. Like deer meat, a wild taste. I don't know what to do to rid that wildness. Did Mr. Lewis tell you anything about soaking it in something to rid that taste?"

"Nope. He just said he didn't want it and my momma could cook it."

"Well, at least he dressed it, so I'll try something." Under her breath, she mumbled something about salt water or vinegar. With a look of resignation, she said, "I'll soak it in salt water overnight and we'll have it for dinner tomorrow."

Next day, about an hour before dinner, Mom removed the duck from the salt soak, washed and seasoned it, and placed the roasting pan in the preheated oven. Over the next hour, its enticing aroma drew us to the kitchen. We could barely wait for the duck to reach doneness.

Dad was still out of town, and the three of us sat at the table. Mom said grace over a mouth-watering roasted bird, then carved portions for each of our plates. A mound of rice and gravy, and a serving of green peas rounded out our meal, and we forked our first bites of duck.

Not a word was spoken among us. Then, violating our mother's strict adherence to manners, Frank discharged a mouthful of duck into his paper napkin. "Yuk." Holding the napkin away from his face, he wiped a hand across his mouth.

Mom stood, went to the sink and rid her bite into the napkin. Turning to me and seeing I still had a mouthful of duck and a face full of distress, she said, "Leave it in your napkin."

Stirring around, she found a can of Spam, sliced it and browned it on top of the stove.

Frank, seemingly enjoying the Spam, asked, "How can duck smell so good and taste so bad? I don't think I'll ever go hunting again, not even if Mr. Lewis wants me to go with him."

Mom smiled. "We don't need wild meat to feed this family, do we?"

Frank and I nodded agreement.

LOVABLE TROUBLE

$\mathscr{S}$KIPPER WAS HIS NAME, BUT it should have been Trouble. Yet, he was the most lovable trouble anyone could want.

Incidents to prove the dichotomy of those statements about our pet would fill a book.

Skipper, a black shorthaired dachshund with rich brown markings on his face, chest, and paws, came to our family as a birthday gift for our eldest son. At the time, we lived in Karachi, Pakistan, not the best place in the world to find a suitable gift for a ten-year-old American kid.

The six-week-old puppy won our son's heart as well as that of the entire family.

Friends returning to the States had already left their Alsatian with us. His name was Rupee, and we treasured this big police dog too. On long walks across the arid area leading to the cricket field behind our house, Skipper trotted along on short little legs, trying to keep up with Rupee. When a pack of wild dogs headed in our direction, Rupee began circling us. His daring way always diverted them in another direction.

Skipper must have learned from Rupee, for he developed his own daredevil personality.

Not long after our puppy came to us, our friends wrote that they missed Rupee. Would we give him back to them and ship him to Alabama?

We took a crated Rupee to the airport and said goodbye to a wonderful animal.

Soon September 1960 arrived, and my husband's military tour in Pakistan ended. We opted to return to the States by ocean liner rather than fly.

We boarded the Italian liner *Victoria* around nine o'clock in the evening. The Buckner family, who gave Skipper to our son, came down to the port to see us off. They said, "Bon voyage," and the ship pulled out past the breakwater at midnight. The kennel had closed when we came aboard. Our four-month-old puppy stayed, by permission, in the stateroom with us that night. First thing the following morning, John took Skipper to the kennel. He returned to tell us that he left our dog yelping loud enough for all the ship's passengers to hear.

On the morning after his first night in the kennel, we headed for breakfast in the dining room when we encountered Skipper and the kennel keeper on deck. He stopped us, and in Italian tried to explain something about our dog while Skipper gulped down something obviously pleasing to his palate. Someone came along and interpreted the keeper's comments. "I'm up all night with this one. He was seasick, and I am feeding him filet mignon. Other kennel animals, they get fish. He gets beef. He's my baby, the youngest in the kennel."

With such good care, we had no worry for Skipper. We visited him several times each day. In the tarp-enclosed area on the deck near the kennel, he showed excitement by bouncing from wall to wall. He yelped the whole time, making such a noise that we cut our visits short.

Time wise, it took a week for the *Victoria* to travel from Karachi to Naples, Italy. Along the water route, we left Skipper and the ship once at a Yemen port and motored inland to Aden. Reaching Italy several days later, we had a five-day layover before boarding the *USS Independence* for New York.

Skipper settled in our Naples hotel, while we planned our visit in this beautiful country.

Next day, John and I, our four children and Skipper sat on the long seat at the back of a coach, ready for an Amalfi Drive excursion. The narrow road skirted the coast south of Naples.

Skipper, content to be with us, showed good behavior on the bus and later, when leashed to a table leg in the inn where we had lunch. Back on the coach, we next unloaded at Pompeii, where his short legs made it through acres of ancient ruins. After several other stops to see quaint fishing villages and the carving of cameos, we arrived back in Naples around dinnertime.

Concrete surfaces around the hotel did not encourage a doggy walk for doing "business." I assumed Skipper tended his need in Pompeii.

Glancing down at him while we waited for my husband to pick up our room key from the desk, I saw our puppy depositing more than a day's accumulation right in the pathway into the dining room.

Jerking his leash, I dragged him upstairs. With tissue and a wet towel, I returned downstairs to do a clean-up job and humble myself before curious stares.

Early the next morning, we took a cab into downtown Naples. Skipper panted from all the walking when I spotted a pet shop and told my husband we needed to buy him a water bowl.

"How do you plan to make them understand you?"

Inside the shop, I pointed to Skipper, stuck out my tongue, panted like a dog, and lapped from my cupped hand as if drinking. The lady shopkeeper grinned, disappeared and returned with a bowl of water for our thirsty dog.

At lunchtime, we found the American Café and again leashed Skipper to the table leg while we enjoyed our first hamburger since leaving the States two years earlier. That evening, our dog rested beneath a restaurant table while we had dinner.

On the third day in Italy, we caught a train heading north, where we planned to board the *USS Independence* in Genoa. Told at the station that our dog did not need a ticket to Rome, we made it to the city without any question of his ridership.

Over our two days in Rome, Skipper toured the Vatican, the Coliseum, and Catacombs, walked the streets and in parks, and rested beneath restaurant tables while we dined.

The fifth day of our visit in Italy, we returned to the rail station, intending to travel on to Genoa with a stop in Florence. "You can't get to Genoa by train," the ticket agent said. "Flooding washed out rails between here and Florence."

We boarded the train back to Naples, and reached within a mile of the station when the conductor walked through our car. Skipper slept beside my husband, and just at that moment, he roused and stretched from a nap. The conductor saw him. "Ah, ticket, please."

My husband pulled out lira, handed it to him, and the man put the money in his pocket.

By the time Skipper turned four months, we had landed back in the States. We owned a spoiled dog who thought he was just another Foster kid. When left home alone, he pulled tissue from the upstairs bathroom and spread it all over the house. We closed the bathroom door, and he pulled Kleenex from the box and deposited tissues all over. The scene resembled a snowfall. With the Kleenex box hidden, we thought the problem solved, but he jumped on tables and knocked off the lamps. He found many ways to show his displeasure when left alone.

The first winter in Maryland, we had a two-foot snowstorm. Skipper romped as well as he could alongside kids on sleds behind our house when two mature German shepherds showed up in our yard. He, showing a daring-do learned from Rupee, attacked the dogs from beneath. He gnawed their under bellies until the shepherds got the upper hand and lopped off part of his ear.

This was first of many trips to the vet. For the week of healing, he endured a bandaged head.

Another of his daring-dos sent my husband and me into a state of angst. On the way home from the navy base, Skipper's head hung out the station wagon's open window, his ears flapping in the breeze. We passed a service station when I turned to see him jump through the window and gallop toward a man walking away from the station toward the sidewalk.

He knocked the man flat on his back on the cement.

My husband pulled over and we ran to help the small man upright and to catch Skipper.

Relief cannot describe our feeling when the man assured us he was not injured, and he even managed to laugh about the whole matter.

There were many more Skipper capers in Maryland, but he had reached the age of four years when we lived on Edwards Air Force Base. On a California summer day, he broke out of the six-foot-high compound wall around our backyard to freedom. Someone left the gate open, allowing him to escape. I discovered him missing and stood on the front driveway calling. Soon, I saw him about a block away. He trotted down the sidewalk at the tail end of a kaboodle of dogs, all trailing the female lead.

As soon as I spotted Skipper, a Military Police vehicle moved in on the pack of dogs. All of them were clearly in violation of the base leash law and in danger of arrest. I had concern for only one of them. "Come on, Skipper!" I yelled in my best cheer leading voice, but he could not make his short little legs run fast enough.

On the corner across the street from our house, the dog-snatching MP nabbed him. Skipper was the only dog in the pack to be arrested.

Devastated, I watched the police vehicle disappear with our dachshund bound for the pound.

With the exception of kennels on the two ocean liners, he had never been separated from us for more than a few hours. I imagined the sound of his hoarse barking during the four-day jail sentence and thought he would make himself sick.

After church on Sunday morning, we drove to the hilltop overlooking the pound. Not daring to allow him to see us, we sat in the car listening to his unmistakable and constant complaints.

Some of us cried, and on Monday morning, I went to rescue him from the calaboose.

Upon seeing me, Skipper's excitement leapt out of control. On the way home, he bounded from the front car seat to the back seat, and to the front again. He showed joy with loud noise, only as a hyperactive dachshund's nature dictated.

There were days when I could have killed him had I not loved him so much. Such as when my husband and I left our younger children in the care of their older brother to attend a party at a friend's home. We received a phone call from our son that Skipper had bitten our youngest son on the mouth. We rushed home to learn our son lay on the floor with Skipper when he decided to blow in the dog's ear.

My husband took our son to the base hospital.

Waiting for them to return, the rest of the family felt concerned about the injured as well as the injurer. Our son came home with stitches, but Skipper could expect quarantine. We put our heads together, thinking of ways to avoid his jail sentence. My husband called the hospital commander, who said there was not a thing he could do. "Anytime an animal bites a person, the rule is fourteen quarantine days."

We cried and cajoled my husband into more phone calls. He went up the chain of command, all the way to the base commander. At last, someone allowed us to keep Skipper confined in our backyard for fourteen days.

After four-plus years at Edwards, my husband had orders to Vietnam, and our family landed back in our Arkansas hometown. The house we purchased had a chain link fence around the back yard, but Skipper dug under the fence to freedom. My husband laid a thick concrete layer beneath the fence line to contain our dog.

He didn't have to break to freedom to leave his legacy. By invitation of the owners of a brown female dachshund, he managed to sire two beautiful puppies in Arkansas.

My husband returned from Vietnam and we returned to Maryland. All of our neighbors on Easy Street knew that Skipper owned the street in front of our house, and they obligingly drove around our aging dog dozing under the sun.

On a 1975 morning, our beloved fourteen-year-old pet tried to rise from his bed after a night's sleep. He could not stand, and we rushed him to the animal hospital. In a few hours, a call came from the veterinarian. "Skipper is fading. If you want to say goodbye, you should come right away."

My husband, our eldest son and I hopped in the car and sped to the hospital. As we tried to tell our precious pet how much joy he brought to our family, the brown dots no longer danced above his sad pained eyes.

ADVENTURES ON THE TIDES

One cold and rainy evening
after dredging all that day,
The cap'n, with his telescope,
saw a policeman far away.

Trim aft your mainsail, Cap'n
and a gambling way we flew,
right down on forbidden ground
to catch a gag or two.

I'll dredge him on the ebb tide;
I'll dredge him on the flood;
I'll dredge him all the winter, and
I'll dredge him in the mud.

I'll feed him bread and water,
give it to him three times a day,
I'll tell you fellows, you're lucky
if ever you get your pay.

LYRICS SUNG BY SOUTHERN MARYLAND watermen defied the lawful order of man in the first half of the Twentieth Century. Before "calming" down in the late 1950s, watermen were the Butch Cassidys and Sundance Kids of the lower Chesapeake Bay and Potomac River. A rough breed, they rode the tides with abandonment.

Early in the morning, I sat with Thomas Shymansky of Cobb Island in a crab house booth looking out on Neale Sound and workboats tied up at the piers. A mist rose from the water, fogging the large glass window. He provided names of other watermen, gave tidbits of information about an older generation on the water, and used the waterman vernacular I would hear later.

"I began going out on the water with my father at age twelve," he said. "I've heard older fishermen tell how 'arstermen' went to Baltimore to hire crewmen. At the end of the season, a boatman arranged to have a sail swing around and knock the crew overboard so they didn't have to pay them for dredging arsters."

This gave me an idea of what I might be hearing in my interviews of other watermen.

I found Garnie Arnold, of Abell, Maryland, feeding ducks on a small pond. A smallish man in stature, he wore a wool pull-on cap and knee-hi boots. Pitching food on the pond's surface, he told stories about his ducks, some of whom had names. With the last handful of scraps thrown, he invited me inside to sit at his dining room table. He, too, was young when he began on the water. "I was eight. I had to go," he said, as though it were a given. "It was that 'in the blood thing.'"

He, like many other watermen, was competitive. Garnie pulled off his green cap and laid it on the table. In 1909 at age sixteen, he borrowed $900 to buy a 75-foot bugeye named *The Blue Wing*. "I learned how to squeeze every possible buck (dollar) out of a boat."

He looked at me as if I might question what he was telling me.

In his bugeye, a sail boat developed in the Chesapeake for dredging oysters, he headed for Baltimore to get a fishing license and to hire a crew.

No one would sign-on with him, saying, "I do not want to go out with a kid." Finally a big Irishman and six others did sign-on, and he headed down to Popular Island with two gallons of whiskey on board. "It was kinda cool and arstering was good."

His boat was out on the water two nights with two dredges working. Each dredge hauled up three to five bushels of oysters every time. On the third day, Garnie doled out a whiskey to each Irishman and headed back to Baltimore with five hundred and twenty-five bushels. "Now, that's a lot of arsters," he said.

Weather came on rough, and the Irish crew began singing, "cause I was taking them home to see sweet Momma. They started to cooking them potatoes and onions and fat bacon. I paid two of them $10, and three of them got $15." Garnie laughed, then sobering said, "Then wages were $12.50 a month. I got a $1.25 a bushel for my arsters right there in the harbor. All illegal, because I dredged out of season, but I was broke before I was paid for the haul and owed money for the bugeye."

Out many a time in the bay or river, he thought he had "put on (his) last clean shirt."

For a small man, there was a certain bravado about Garnie. He told about taking out a fishing party of three. They were "lit up with liquor and began fighting and tearing up the life preservers." They threw the tiller overboard, and Garnie used a broomstick to guide the boat back into shore.

He replaced the tiller, and near the end of World War I on April 13, 1918, a New York newspaper reporter hired Garnie to take him out to the bay's mid channel. The newswire reported a German merchant ship headed for the Baltimore port. It was Good Friday, Garnie remembered. *The Deutschland* supposedly carried a load of cloth dye. He anchored off Sharp's Island, and they waited. "The reporter got me drunk, then he said, 'When the *Dutchland* (sic) comes along, we're going to board her so I can get pictures.'"

Garnie was not so drunk that he didn't know a good deal when he ran head-on into one. "I didn't tell Mr. Reporter that the German ship had already gone past us. A really big snowstorm was coming down and those big old channel boats were plowing through to port. He was paying me $2.50 an hour overtime. I would have stayed out there as long as he wanted for that money."

Years later, Garnie and other watermen ran their boats at illegal times in illegal waters and used illegal methods to harvest oysters, crabs, rockfish, and bluefish. Oyster Wars on the Potomac flared between Maryland and Virginia in the 1950s. It was like "hell was a-popping."

A prelude for the wars came down in the 1600s under the Maryland Charter. England's king granted Lord Calvert control of the Potomac River to the edge of the Virginia shore. In other words, the river belonged to the colony of Maryland.

In a 1785 compact, the two colonies agreed that neither could interfere with the other's trade or fishing on the river. They agreed to allow each other free access on the Chesapeake Bay and Potomac River.

In 1877, an agreement between the two states set the boundary line at the low water mark on the Virginia side but granted embayments (water between points of land jutting into the river). The Matthews-Nelson Survey in 1927 set this line as a fixed boundary.

When Maryland and Virginia watermen turned violent in the 1950s over rights to oyster beds and other bay and river resources, both states armed patrol vessels. The Oyster Wars began.

They continued until a 1958 agreement established the Potomac River Fisheries Commission defining the power of enforcement within its jurisdictional boundaries. (Source: www.virginiaplaces.org/boundaries/mdboundary.html).

If in the early years watermen found high adventure on the Chesapeake, in the '50s, it became "battles most every night on the lower Potomac." At the time, Virginians were denied Potomac fishing and oyster dredging rights. Later, dredging to harvest oysters was outlawed for conservation reasons, and tonging adopted as the legal method.

Maryland's Free State and Virginia's Old Dominion lawmakers argued their cases as watermen and marine patrols duked it out in a game of "lure the police."

Wherever the numerous creeks and rivers emptied into the two larger bodies of water, forming spits of land such as Stump Neck, Cedar Point Neck, Cobb Island, and Colton's Point, watermen with names such as Sayre, Shymansky, and Robrecht worked their boats and grew their legends. Their battles became fodder for repeated tales around the pot-bellied stove in general stores.

On St. George's Island, hardened sailors salted their adventures with distinct Maryland accents and watermen's vernacular, peppered with plenty of laughter.

On a winter day, an old sailor tilted his straight back chair on two legs and began his story. He saw this big fast boat belonging to a Virginian set out for a night of dredging near St. George's Creek when a light aluminum police boat came out of nowhere. "It's so dark the helmsman can barely see that big boat. That old Virginian lets the light boat catch up almost to his big boat, then, he eases a little ways farther out into the river and stops. The marine cozies up close to him again, and that old waterman eases out a little more." This keeps up, the waterman said, until the lone patrol officer finds he is pretty far out in his small, light boat. It strikes him that the Virginian might have an idea to swamp him, and the patrol officer pulls his gun.

"All of a sudden here comes that big old Virginian's boat barreling down on him, swerving past and splashing an uphill avalanche across that light boat. He flaunted his dredge from the boom and left that marine as limp as a dishrag."

The general store room filled with roars of laughter. The waterman stands up, and struts around the stove, slapping his thigh with his seaman's cap.

The room settled down, and a stocky, unshaven waterman, still wearing a short waterproof jacket despite the heat radiating from the stove, said he had a story about another old Virginian. His Virginia waterman allowed the patrol boat to catch up and tie onto the stern of his big powerful fishing boat. The fish harvester looked back and yelled that he was too busy to talk because he had to haul in his nets, and asked the patrol to let him finish. "Well, he finished and walked to the back of his boat, looked that marine squarely in the eye and said, 'Now Cap'n, I'm gonna put my bow over in Virginia. What you gonna do there at the stern?' That policeman had just two choices, to cut loose or be towed off."

Waiting for the laughter to subside, another waterman leaned back on two chair legs before he chimed in. "Once, I'll tell you, you would a thought hell was a-popping on the Potomac. It was nigh onto evening tide and time for them Maryland dredgers to surface. Cap'n Cheseldine . . . you know, he was a marine policeman who knew the river so well that when fog set down low and thick as pea soup, they said he would just lift up the fog so he could see under it."

On one foggy night, the captain gave part of his crew orders to take *The Kent*, their patrol boat, on to its Cobb Island berth. In this ploy, *The Kent* set up a decoy for the illegal dredgers to see while Captain Cheseldine and his first mate waited at the old bathhouse near Morgantown. "It wasn't long before them dredgers slipped out after them arsters."

When the skipjack—another Maryland work boat under sails—eased in front of the two patrolmen at the bathhouse, "the lawmen started throwing ammo into them. Bullets peppered all around. Them two hefties rolled back in their boat, but you know what? Several of the lawmen's bullets sliced the dredge line and all the evidence fell down to the river bottom."

Laughter bounced around the room again.

Following a silent spell, a younger, quieter watermen asked, "Why didn't that Marylander use one of those big old butcher knives he carried under the washboard—a ledge around the inside of a boat—to cut that evidence loose? Police caint do anything without the evidence."

A yarn spinner leaned back in his chair and gave the young man a look of disbelief. "Yeah, well he didn't wanna lose his haul." Then, he recalled a night when the police came upon some dredgers and the police cut loose with machine guns blazing and boats running wide open. "All they managed to kill was three cows on the river bank."

This drew gales of guffaws and when they ebbed, another old codger told of the physical stress in trying to out-fox the marine police. "Why I wore my teeth off holding the hook of a flashlight between them so I could cull arsters with both hands." To save his teeth and the place where he fished, he rigged a buoy. He put a board across an inner tube, attached a basket with a lantern beneath it. The buoy marked his fishing spot and allowed light for culling. "The police couldn't see that kind of light," he said

Some of his fellow workers expressed doubt that such a light could escape police detection. This caused heavy silence around the potbelly stove until one storyteller turned to another. "Do you know that the three worst things in the world are a leaky boat, a stove that smokes, and a fussy wife? Damned if I don't have all three."

A few groans slipped through the lips of some who had heard the three worst things many times. Still, it stirred a ripple of laughter, when a seasoned man of the water said, "What have you to say, George?"

Finally, the quiet one had an opening. "What if the police had a little help finding you?" he asked. "Once I didn't come in from running the arster beds when my wife expected me." He blushed deep red. "We'd just been married bout six months. She sent the police out to look for me. It cost me sixty bucks in fines for an illegal catch."

His tale brought the house down as he scratched his head and settled back in his chair.

His cohort in crime chided him. "Didn't I tell you bout the three worst things in the world, and one of them is a fussy wife?"

Another oft-repeated tale showed how watermen tried to assist each other in avoiding the marine police. An old salt said in a big roundup in 1955, he was the only waterman on St. George's Island not fishing one night when he heard of the patrol's plans. Jumping into his boat, he went around warning everyone fishing. Pulling off his wool cap, he readjusted it on his head, and said, "We was all standing along the island bridge, watching spook-like as the police threw their search lights all around, peering for us vanished watermen."

Each outwitting-the-law caper brought laughter from those around the stove.

The clever watermen proved they knew many ways to out-smart law enforcement. They did not always win when pitting their wits against law and nature, but more often than not, they sneaked past marine patrols and eked out a labor-intensive but comfortable living.

The 1958 compact settled fishing rights, and the marine police cracked down on enforcement. The best the watermen could remember, the last big roundup happened in 1960.

Today, Southern Maryland watermen fight their battles through the state legislature. They tong for oysters from Labor Day, through long icy winters and up to the month of May. They crab and fish, then Labor Day comes around again and the tonging begins for another season. Each season holds eternal hope of a better catch than the last one. Despite the odds and their diminishing numbers, watermen continue to have respect for their trade and believe "it's just in the blood."

To their dismay, it is not in the blood of many of their sons.

The watermen around that potbellied stove lamented the fact that their sons shy away from a lifestyle they inherited from their fathers. Perhaps, the appeal to a younger generation slipped away with the end of high adventures in the late '50s.

Much of the color, the fire and spit, the very ginger that kept their adrenaline flowing and made a waterman adventurous sailed into port with their skipjacks. Now, the once hearty sailors sit around the general stores in waterfront communities, ballyhooing about their long-ago capers. Their oft-swapped tales make them heroes, and while they may not find life as exciting as yesteryear, they will continue to

Tong on the ebb tide,
Tong on the flood,
They will tong all the winter,
And tong in the mud.

IN MEMORY OF OZZIE AND HARRIET

*I*T WAS THE TENTH FAMILY Christmas gathering at Windwood, Maha and Paha's home in Maryland. The wished-for snow went north that year. There would be no afternoon sledding down the steep hill behind the house. The slope ran the length of two football fields to the edge of the two-acre pond.

Sledding brought the height of winter excitement to Windwood. Maha marked the bone-chilling activity off the holiday agenda, and without it decided there would be no hot chocolate heating on the kitchen stovetop. She knew groans of disappointment would be heard but anticipated other Christmas joys. Instead of chocolate, she had cider to offer.

Soon all four adult children, their wives and six grandchildren came bearing loads of gifts, stories to tell, and laughter to share. Family stories became repeats of the many comical situations the military family had experienced. Three daughters-in-law and a son-in-law endured the telling and retelling with social grace. They often contributed to a story and laughed as much as the insiders did. Maha and Paha felt gifted to have such a fine family.

During this Maryland Christmas without snow, it came time to open gifts. Everyone knew how to provide pleasant surprises, and Paha got the biggest surprise of all. His gift was not under the tree. It wasn't even wrapped, and he had to go outdoors to receive it.

His youngest son, David and wife Karen handed him a cage. Ozzie and Harriet, two white domesticated geese peeped out at Paha. "The geese spook the horses in the arena. I can't risk a student injury during riding lessons. We must get them off the farm," Karen said.

New Era Farm Riding School horses and boarded animals were at risk too.

Thrilled with his live gift, Paha said his pond was the perfect home for the beautiful waterfowl.

He penned them in the barn for several days to make them acquainted with their new surroundings. Then on a sunny morning, he secured a long stick and herded Ozzie and Harriet down Windwood's long lane to the pond. He returned, laughing, and told Maha, "They took to the water like a duck. Waddled right into the pond. I will go get them before dark. I don't want an owl or some other bird of prey to get them."

Through the rest of the winter, spring and fall, Paha walked Ozzie and Harriet to the pond each morning. Some mornings Maha joined them, and she and Paha sat on a grassy knoll watching the two geese pluck tender blades of grass. The geese made a game of untying their sneaker laces. Standing by while the strings were retied, they seemed to get a real bang out of untying them a second and third time.

Once the game was over, Ozzie became protective of Harriet. He plucked a few blades of grass, lifted his head on a long graceful neck and peered around while she ate constantly in the knowledge of his guardianship. Tiring of the shoe game and eating grass, Harriet followed Ozzie into the water and they floated around all day.

On the mornings when Maha went to the pond with them, Harriet "pucked" along beside her. "Puck, puck, puck," she sounded the extent of her vocabulary. Maha responded, "Puck, puck, puck."

So the conversation went down the hill, until Ozzie exercised an unpleasant goose quirk. With a yen for showing his custodial role of protecting Harriet, he fell behind Maha, intending to nip her in the rear end. Head lowered and hissing, he aimed for the target.

Paha put his herding stick beside Ozzie's long neck to hold off the attack.

Maha was never nipped, but that did not mean the end of Ozzie's devilment if he thought to try again. Thinking he showed off for Harriet's sake, Maha said Harriet paid no attention to Ozzie's swashbuckling act. "She just waddles alongside, puck, puck, pucking contentment."

In early spring, the geese built a large nest on a small island in the pond. Completed, Harriet laid eggs and set on them.

Ozzie kept a watchful lookout.

Paha did not try to get them to leave the pond at night, even though he and Maha worried a snake or some preying fowl or animal would steal the eggs and the geese. One morning about three weeks later, when Paha checked on them, he heard gosling noises coming from the island nest. Some days later, he and Maha witnessed a string of goslings trailing behind Harriet, while Ozzie floated ahead, beside, or behind in his protective mode.

Then one night it happened. Everyone of the baby flock fell prey to a nocturnal predator.

Paha and Maha dealt with their sadness.

Soon Christmastime was a month away. The snow came early. Two-feet fell over several days. Before dark, Paha brought the geese home to the safety of the barn.

Ozzie must have felt it was a goose's kind of weather. That night he led Harriet back to the pond.

In falling snow next morning, Paha discovered them missing and went looking for them. He returned with a handful of white feathers. "Blood and feathers strewn all around this side of the pond," he said. "I found spent shells. Unlawful trespassers shot them. Guess someone will have a good Thanksgiving dinner."

Maha wiped a tear from her cheek. "Well, while we had them, those two amazing birds provided a year full of wonderful memories. Let's get ready for the family's arrival. They will want to hit the sleds right away. Don't let me forget to make the hot chocolate."

CONAN AND PRINCESS

WHEN SKIPPER, OUR FOURTEEN-YEAR-OLD DACHSHUND, died in 1975, I swore, "No more pets will worm a path into my heart with their unconditional love."

Hm-m, swearings often fall by the wayside, just as promises have a way of unraveling.

A few years had passed after we lost Skipper when a beautiful cat found us. My husband came from the barn to tell me about him. "He's black and white with yellow patches. A real pretty cat and he looks like he's been well cared for."

"John, you know we said no more pets. We can't take them with us when we travel, and I don't like to leave them at the kennel. No more pets, and that's final."

I thought I sounded determined, then John said he didn't know what would happen to the cat if he wasn't fed. "He will starve. I'll make him a place to sleep in the barn."

I sighed and gave in. "Oh well, let him stay. Feed him but be sure he stays at the barn. I do not want to become attached. You can name him Barney."

Six months Barney stayed in the barn, never seen by me. Then ready to leave in the car one day, I found him in the garage. Not wanting to close him inside, I picked the cat up, intending to return him to the barn.

Barney gave a painful meow and jumped from my hands.

"You gorgeous cat, you are quite pregnant," I muttered. "Well, we will call you Barnette." Animals are easy conversers. Ears twitch, eyes stare straight into your eyes, and they never talk back.

151

I inched toward attachment as Barnette edged away with a leery look behind.

She returned to the barn and continued to bed there, but before long, I saw her in the garage again. John returned her several times more to her lofty house with carpeted floor and walls. We thought it the perfect place to birth her litter, but it became obvious that Barnette did not think so. She appeared more and more around our house.

Then on Easter morn, when Maryland's April weather dawned quite cool, John found her and six pretty kittens on a bed of dry leaves in a window well. One kitten was dead.

The same morning, our four families arrived for Easter dinner and an egg hunt. Barnette and the kittens became the main attraction, winning the hearts of all our animal lovers. Our grandchildren helped John build a cardboard shield around and over Barnette's chosen abode.

Back in their homes, phone calls came frequently. "How are the cats?"

"Barnette's content for now, but soon her babies will be old enough to move, kit and kaboodle, back to the barn," John told a grandchild.

Shortly, he did move our cat family back to the barn, then one morning he came to the house with bad news. "A varmint strew things all over the place and killed another kitten—the prettiest one, a patchwork calico."

I was devastated even while striving for detachment, and at the next family gathering, I pronounced, "Soon they are off to another home, the Humane Society kennel."

"You know what will happen?" Our daughter-in-law appealed to a near-melting heart. "You have four kittens left. We," she said, speaking for our son too, "will take two to our horse farm if you will keep the other two. We get first pick. That black one. We'll call him Pirate, and the gray one is Butter Bean." Accustomed to finding names for her riding school horses, she had no trouble tagging her new animals.

Her decision left a black male kitten with a white blaze on his chest and a patchwork princess as pretty as peaches. We watched them grow a while longer, observing their personalities. It became obvious that the male was a daredevil and attacked the sweet, loving female in fits of jealousy. If she could not avoid him, she ran from him. We had one hell-raiser, the other gentle and lovable—two distinct personalities. We loved both of them, and named the devil maker, Conan. The gentle one, we appropriately called, Princess.

Conan's name did not come without debate. I thought Beast a better tag for him, but John won out. I had to agree, either name suited him.

Several months old, our Conan climbed a tall pine tree and did not know how to back his way down. He meow-ed his distress, and John brought out the ladder for the rescue.

A real little beast, he surprised us when it became evident he was a mama's boy too. At six months old, he still tried to nurse Barnette. For a time, she lay on the deck in the sun and let him have his way. Then, one day we noticed our beautiful mother cat was missing. Calling did not bring her to us. Days passed, and still no Barnette. Finally, we concluded an owl or some other predator snatched her from the barn.

We grieved our loss, and months went by, when one day on our walk we saw a beautiful cat in our neighbor's yard. "That looks like Barnette. That is Barnette!"

We dialed our neighbor and asked about the cat. "Oh yes, she just showed up here. We named her Pearl. She's a great house cat." Henry filled us in on his trip to the vet. "He had prepped her when he turned to us and said, 'She's already been fixed.'"

Henry was surprised when we claimed our cat who was neutered after her kittens were born.

During our conversation, we nodded agreement that Henry and Alice should keep Pearl. "She will be one confused cat if she undergoes one more name change," John said.

Barnette proved she had a mind of her own, and I suspected that Conan inherited the gene from his mother.

After Barnette's departure, Conan and Princess hung out at the house more and more. Soon, they charmed us into a slanted walk-up to a double deck, garage condominium complete with carpeted walls and floor. In winter, each had a heating pad to ward off the cold. With them underfoot, I became totally attached, and we enjoyed a few more wonderful years with them in our adopted state of Maryland.

Then in September 2001, we placed them in large carriers on the backseat of the car and made the two-day trip to Arkansas. "Princess will meow all the way," I said, but she made not a peep. It was Conan who me-eowed all morning on the first day of travel.

Parking under a shade tree, we rolled down the windows and went for lunch. When we returned to the car, both were asleep. It was not until our three-vehicle, moving caravan broke up that the cats and I had a real conversation. Well, sort of.

The sun dropped below the horizon right before we reached Knoxville. I followed in the car with the cats behind the Penske truck when it exited I-40 and soon realized the driver had pulled into a weight station. I circled around behind the station to avoid the scale.

John and his cousin, the Penske driver, had cell phones. My only communication was with Conan and Princess. When I exited the weight station back onto I-40, neither the Penske truck nor John's loaded white Toyota truck was in sight.

"Okay," I told the cats, "I can trek through Knoxville blindfolded." I might as well have been blindfolded. It was a moonless night.

The cats did not make a sound, but it was comforting just to have them with me.

We plowed ahead at top speed in an effort to catch up with the rest of the caravan. Just before reaching Cookville, where we had lodging reservations, I spotted John's truck pulled into the exit lane of another weight station. Slowing, I allowed the two trucks to get out ahead of me.

"Well," I told the cats, "I could do without the kind of uncertainty we've had tonight, but I sure am glad I had you along for the ride."

That evening in the motel, sandbox used, Conan and Princess made themselves at home, seemingly happy just to be with us.

The next day they claimed Arkansas as their home.

All was happiness with our beloved cats, until several years ago when both, within a month of each other, went to the Rainbow Gate where they wait for us.

WHEN TEACHER IS A FRIEND

*S*HE HAD THE FACE OF an English bulldog and a will of steel.

That is the way we, Miss Walker's students, chose to see her. Only in later years did I come to see the beauty in that face and the way she carried herself with determination. Her determined goal was for us to learn proper English grammar and read books having permanent value, emotional effect and excellent form.

A few years ago in her eighties, she grew tired of fighting the debilitating Parkinson's Disease and died. The disease did not keep her from agreeing to read a draft of my nearly completed first novel. As I fed manuscript pages to her, she read them, made suggestions and corrections, and encouraged me to keep at it. "Yours is the kind of book I like to read," she wrote in one of her long letters. Her tiny, hard-to-read handwriting was still familiar from my high school years.

Through years of correspondence with her, I kept up with classmates, all of whom spent four years in her English classes. All of her classes consisted of no more than twenty to twenty-five members. Many students from our small school went on to notable achievements, in no small measure, because of Miss Walker.

Students did not make her job easy. There was the "rowdy" class of seniors, one year ahead of us. The rowdy class had more boys than girls. When teacher left them unattended, the boys chewed huge wads of paper into spitballs. When the balls were hard and tight, the boys began an all-out spitball battle that had the girls in their class diving beneath their desks. I know this because I married one of those boys.

One day, Miss Walker came through the door just as a spitball slammed into the doorframe near her head. She stopped dead still in the doorway and stared down the boys with that face. The English bulldog look. Her gaze was so effective that it ended the game in her classroom. The rowdy class graduated from eleventh grade and moved its battle across the hall to the science teacher's room. There they exchanged spitballs for chalk erasers.

Miss Walker did not have a problem with my docile class. Perhaps a reason for this rested in numbers and gender. Our class consisted of fifteen girls and only five boys. Or maybe the bulldog face challenged us from day one.

Our beloved teacher never married. As far as we knew, she never dated. The girls in our class speculated about that state of affairs and determined it was the reason she never smiled.

When Miss Walker walked into the classroom, back unbending, looking straight ahead, it was all business. We got the message even before she said, "Turn to page thirty-five in your workbooks and diagram the sentences." Today, she would use "parse" the sentences.

Six months of our school term, she taught grammar. The other three, we read literature. I think most of the class had a strong disregard for Shakespeare. It was difficult for us with a southern dialect to comprehend the Sixteenth Century English bard. Torture did not describe the fear of standing before the class to give an oral book review of three to five minutes duration, or to recite a poem. One thought Miss Walker would grow weary of such torture, but she hung with us.

We learned proper grammar, and through literature, we learned how other cultures viewed the world. It took time for us to realize the dedication this beloved teacher gave to her profession.

Some of her remarks stayed with me over the years. From some class reading we were into at the time, she asked, "What is happiness?"

We gave such definitions as, "Happiness is when you aren't hurting." "It's enjoying something or someone." "It's when you're smiling."

After allowing us to mull over the word and its meaning, she said, "All of your answers are right. There are things you need to know about happiness. It is a fleeting emotion. Sometimes, you must work to attain a happy mood. When you have moments of happiness, treasure them. When they pass, anticipate more down the road." She said there would always be happiness in our lives. It just would not hang around as a permanent thing.

All through our high school years, Miss Walker did not look happy. At retirement age, she left teaching and became the school librarian. On brief visits with her, when returning to my hometown, I began to notice the changed look on her face. It softened into radiant smiles of contentment—perhaps happiness. She was beautiful.

Miss Walker made a lasting mark on my life and took an endearing place in my heart. I concluded that my teacher, my friend, came to realize a man in her life was not necessary for her happiness.

CPSIA information can be obtained at www.ICGtesting.com
Printed in the USA
LVOW062356030112

262262LV00003B/3/P